# HEARTS AGAINST ODDS

## COLIN BRADLEY

CB
BOOKS

www.colinbradleybooks.com

First Edition

Edited by: Cindy Draughon
Book Cover & Interior Design by: Brad Thomas

ISBN 979-8-9935597-0-4 (Paperback)
ISBN 979-8-9935597-1-1 (Hardback)

Published by CB Books
www.colinbradleybooks.com

# DEDICATION

To the men and women of the United States Military and to all first responders your courage, sacrifice, and unyielding service stand as a beacon of strength and hope.

In remembrance of September 11, 2001, may we never forget the lives lost, the heroes who answered the call, and the resilience that continues to unite us.
This book is for you.

# ACKNOWLEDGMENTS

My heartfelt thanks to my editor, whose insight and dedication shaped this story into its best form. To my family and friends, your unwavering support and encouragement sustained me through every draft. To the beta readers, your thoughtful feedback and keen eyes helped refine each page. I am deeply grateful to each of you this book would not exist without your belief in it and in me.

# CHAPTER ONE

*T*he year was 2000, and the town nestled among the backroads of Southern Illinois farmland was quiet. Here, football games filled Friday nights, coffee was always plentiful at the diner, and everyone knew each other's business long before it was shared. Trevor walked across the stage in his black cap and gown and shook hands and posed for pictures with a smile, but the weight on his shoulders felt heavier than it should have with a high school diploma in his hand.

For four years, teachers, family, and even people he didn't know at the grocery store had told him the same thing: "Go to college. Do something with your life." The words had turned into background noise, like the sound of cicadas in July. He never got any scholarships and he was turned down for the Pell Grant he applied for, and even though he never told anyone, Trevor wasn't sure if he had the discipline or the brains to get through college.

Most of his friends had already written the next chapter of their life. They were packing up and leaving for campuses all over the state, some as close as Carbondale and others as far away as Champaign. Trevor stayed behind and looked down at a stack of overdue bills on the kitchen counter. Most of them came from the cars and trucks he bought on a whim in high school. Each one was shinier than the last and was a desperate attempt to get attention. He thought a flashy car would get people to notice and respect him. Instead, it left him broke, and creditors were calling.

At night, he wore the stiff polo shirt of the Lake Front Café and worked under buzzing fluorescent lights that sounded like angry bees. As the line cook, a dead-end job he'd stumbled into to cover mounting bills, Trevor spent his nights flipping burgers. At the end of every late shift his feet ached... and he asked himself: Is this worth it?

Trevor knew deep down this wasn't the life he was meant to have. He wasn't supposed to be defined by the smell of fryer grease and the flicker of fluorescent lights. As a boy, he ran through the tall grass behind his house with a stick for a rifle. He always thought something bigger was waiting for him just beyond the horizon. He wanted to be a hero, to stand up for something bigger than himself, and to live a life that required bravery and gave meaning to sacrifice.

He had no money, no plans, and a nagging feeling that ahead on the path was failure. It seemed painfully clear. He considered the military. It wasn't just a way to get out of debt or out of the county. He could burn away his doubts and show himself that he could become the man he had always wanted to be.

The Army recruiting office was in a run-down strip mall between a pawn shop and a place that gave out payday loans.

The glass door rattled when Trevor opened it, and the smell of old coffee and floor polish hit him. He stepped inside, and his nerves buzzed under a calm facade.

A man with broad shoulders and pressed fatigues looked up from behind the desk. His name tag identified him as Grant. The staff sergeant shook hands firmly and smiled in a way that was both friendly and calculating. He pointed to the chair across from his desk.

"Take a seat," Grant said as he pulled a thick stack of forms out of a drawer.

The questions came in quick succession. History of health issues and surgeries he'd had as well as injuries, illnesses, or sexually transmitted diseases. Trevor moved around in the plastic chair and the pen made a noise as it went across the pages. He had imagined something different. The man had given no inspiring speeches, no talk of bravery or brotherhood. Just some forms. "When will we get to the good stuff?" he thought, jaw clenched.

When Trevor signed the last page he leaned forward, his voice full of determination. He said, "I'd like a job that matters. Something that lets me see the world."

Grant laughed and leaned back in his chair. "That depends. First, we need to see how well you do on the ASVAB. That will let us know what jobs you can get.

Another test. Trevor made himself nod, but inside he was angry. Once again, his future came down to numbers on a piece of paper.

Grant pushed a pair of old study guides across the desk.

"Take a look at these. Do the work, and everything will be fine."

Trevor took them home like holy books, with his future written between their pages. Every night after work he sat hunched over the kitchen table with a highlighter in one hand and a cup of coffee in the other, until long past midnight. Words turned into equations, and diagrams of machines turned into practice tests. His eyes were sore by the end of the week, but his determination was stronger than ever.

He went back to Grant. "I'm ready."

Trevor's heart raced in time with his footsteps as he walked into the testing center the next morning. There were many nervous people in the room, and the young men and women were shifting in their seats, each holding on to their hopes.

The first part was Trevor's weak point: English. The questions felt like quicksand, and every sentence seemed like it would pull him under, but he kept going. He took deep breaths, forced himself to pay attention, and kept his pencil moving. He fought through section after section, hour after hour. He leaned back in his chair and felt drained after the test. He didn't feel like he had won, but he also didn't feel like he had lost. He just felt worried.

He knew that the Combat Aptitude score was the most important number. To be a Cavalry Scout, he had to get at least an 87.

"How did it go?" Grant asked.

"Great," Trevor said with a smile that didn't reach his

eyes.

Grant put the papers in a folder and said, "We'll know tomorrow. Come back in the morning and we'll talk about the results."

That night was a long, painful wait. Trevor couldn't sleep. The heat in his room felt stale and he kept going over every question in his head. In the dark, each wrong guess got bigger. His body was worn out by morning, but his willpower got him up and into the recruiter's office.

Grant looked at the score sheet, his face blank. Seconds felt like hours. At last he looked up and tapped the paper, his words coming out slowly. "You did well in arithmetic reasoning, mechanical comprehension, and auto & shop information. That gives you an 88 for Combat."

Trevor's chest got tight. His heart raced against his ribs. Does that mean...?

Finally, Grant said, "Congratulations," and his face broke into a big smile that made it look less hard. "Your scores were good enough to be a cavalry scout in the best part of the military."

Trevor let out a breath he hadn't realized he had been holding, and a wave of relief washed over him. His shoulders dropped and he smiled. "Did I? That's wonderful. Thanks, Sergeant."

Grant raised a hand, and his face went from beaming to serious. "Don't get too excited yet. You still have to pass your physical at MEPS in St. Louis." He leaned over the desk and spoke more quietly. "Be honest with me. Do you take drugs?"

Trevor said, "No" very quickly, almost too swiftly. He sat up straight in his chair. "I only smoke cigarettes sometimes."

"That won't be a problem. You just have to pass a drug test." Grant slapped the desk hard and stood up, ending the conversation as quickly as it had started. "Scout, I'll see you in two weeks."

Trevor heard the word "Scout" over and over again in his head as he drove back to his parents' house, adrenaline still pumping through his body. He could already see himself in combat boots and a pressed uniform with the title sewn on his chest. His new identity was taking shape. He could hardly sit still by the time he got to the gravel drive.

Trevor called his parents into the kitchen that night. As his father pulled out a chair, the familiar oak table creaked. His mother put down the dish towel she had been holding, her eyes already guarded. They could feel how serious he was.

Trevor sat across from them, his palms slick against the smooth wood. The words were stuck in his throat, heavy as a rock. He thought about it for a second, looking for the right opening, but nothing came to mind. Finally, he just let it out.

"I signed up with the Army," he said, his voice steadier than he felt. "I'm going to be a Cavalry Scout. In two months,

I'll be shipping out to Fort Knox, Kentucky."

There was silence. During the pause, the clock in the kitchen ticked loudly, and each second seemed to stretch like a rope pulled tight. His parents looked at him with wide eyes, as if he had just spoken in a different language.

His dad said, "Good grief," and leaned back, rubbing his face with his hand. He looked at Trevor's mom. She shook her head and pressed her lips together tightly.

At last, she let out a breath. "Okay," she said softly, as if she were being careful. "Tell us more."

Trevor leaned forward, happy to have the chance. Words came out in a hurry. He talked about the training, the career path, and the signing bonus. He talked about the stability, the benefits, and the future he could make. He told them how it would be good for him, good for them, and good for everyone. He pitched it like a salesman trying to make a sale, hoping that if he believed it hard enough, they would too.

But their faces stayed flat and still.

His dad let out a long sigh and set his hands firmly on the table. "Okay, Trevor," he said, his voice carrying a careful balance of pride and worry. "I want to support you in this— but I need to know you really understand what you're getting into." He paused, his eyes narrowing with quiet seriousness. "Once you sign on, there's no backing out. If you quit, they'll call it AWOL, and you could end up in jail. This isn't a game." After a moment, he added, "I'd also like to meet this recruiter of yours. I want to hear directly what you're stepping into."

Trevor nodded quickly, more to ease the tension than because he wanted to think about the warning. "Okay, Dad. I understand." I gave a hint of a smile, but it felt like it was going to break. *At least they didn't blow up. Things could have been worse.*

He knew it wasn't over when he pushed back from the table and headed to his room, the air still heavy with unspoken words. His parents might have let the conversation drop for now, but he could tell they hadn't come to terms with his enlistment. Nor had they truly accepted it.

In the hallway, Trevor stopped at the house phone mounted on the wall. He picked up the receiver, the cord curling against his arm as he dialed Staff Sergeant Grant's number from memory. When Grant answered, Trevor asked if he would be willing to come by the house and talk things through with his parents face-to-face.

"Of course," Grant said without hesitation. "I'll be there tomorrow morning."

Trevor replaced the receiver, then walked back into the kitchen where his parents still sat, silent with their coffee cups. "Staff Sergeant Grant's coming here tomorrow," he told them quietly. "He wants to sit down with you both and answer any questions."

His mom and dad exchanged a glance, uncertain, but neither protested. That was enough. For the first time all evening, Trevor felt a sliver of relief, maybe tomorrow they'd finally hear what he already knew: that this was the right step forward.

Trevor lay in bed that night, looking at the little cracks in the ceiling and listening to the old fan creak above him. His chest felt tight, and it wasn't just because of the August date on his papers. The thought broke through for the first time since he signed that it wasn't just about when and where he was going. It was about all the things and people he would leave behind.

The next morning, the doorbell rang right on time. Trevor's parents exchanged a look before Trevor opened the door to find Staff Sergeant Grant, his Army recruiter, standing tall in his uniform. He had offered to come by the house after Trevor signed his enlistment papers, knowing his parents still had questions.

They gathered in the living room, Trevor on the couch beside his mom, his dad sitting stiffly in his recliner across from Grant. The tension was unmistakable.

His father cleared his throat. "So, it's official, then. He's already signed?"

Trevor nodded. "Yes, Dad."

Grant spoke up, his voice steady but reassuring. "That's right, sir. Trevor has enlisted as a Cavalry Scout. I wanted to come by to make sure you both had a clear picture of what that means and why it's a good fit for him."

His mom folded her hands tightly in her lap. "All we keep hearing is 'scout for the cavalry.' That doesn't tell us much. What will he actually be doing out there?"

Grant leaned forward slightly, his tone respectful. "That's a fair question. A Cavalry Scout is the Army's eyes and ears. They go ahead of the main force, gather intelligence, and report back. Scouts use advanced optics, communication systems, navigation equipment, you name it. They're not just wandering into danger blindly. They're trained to move smart, observe, and provide the information that keeps the rest of the unit safe."

His father frowned. "Sounds risky."

Grant didn't flinch. "Every Army role carries some level of risk. But Scouts are some of the most thoroughly trained soldiers we have. Trevor will go through rigorous instruction in reconnaissance, surveillance, and small-unit tactics. He'll learn to work with a team and to use his head as much as his hands. That training gives him an edge both in and out of the military."

His mother's voice was softer, almost pleading. "But what happens after? What about when he comes home?"

Grant's expression warmed. "Ma'am, the Army doesn't just give him a uniform. It gives him a foundation. He'll have the GI Bill for college, VA benefits, healthcare, and job training. Employers value Cavalry Scouts because they're problem-solving men and women who can handle stress, adapt quickly, and lead others. Whether Trevor makes this a career or decides to transition back to civilian life, he'll have skills and opportunities that put him ahead."

The room quieted. His parents didn't look thrilled, but the rigid worry in their posture eased into something closer to acceptance.

"You really think he's cut out for this?" his father asked at last.

Grant nodded without hesitation. "Yes, sir. Trevor has the drive and the mindset to succeed. The Scout program will challenge him, but it will also bring out the best in him. I've seen young men like him step into this role and grow into leaders. I have no doubt he'll do the same."

Trevor watched his parents exchange a glance. For the first time since signing the papers, he felt the tension in the room lift, just slightly. His parents might not be ready to celebrate, but at least they were beginning to see that his decision wasn't a reckless leap into the unknown, it was a step into something solid.

When Trevor told his closest friends, they all reacted with a stunned silence and then disbelief.

One of Trevor's friends finally spoke, shaking his head. "Are you kidding me?"

"No," Trevor said, his voice calm but firm. "I'm serious. I'm going into the Army."

They laughed and shook their heads as if it were a cruel joke. "You're going to regret it, man. In college, there are a lot more girls than in the Army. You'll miss out."

Trevor smirked, but didn't pay any attention to what they said. They might have been right in their own way. He might miss out. But something inside him told him this was the right and necessary thing to do.

His friends weren't going to let the moment end on such a serious note. "Okay, then. We need to throw a party if you're really going. "Send you off right."

Trevor laughed, both relieved and nervous. He knew they would never really get it until they dealt with the same restlessness that was eating away at them. Still, a party seemed like the best way to celebrate the end of one life and the start of another.

Trevor's friends kept their word that weekend. They all met at his neighbor's cabin by the river, which had seen a lot of late-night bonfires and summer memories over the years. When he pulled up, strings of lights lit up the yard and the dark river, and the headlights bouncing off the gravel drive showed trucks and cars parked along the tree line. He hadn't expected this. It looked like half the town was here. The music was so loud the windows shook, and he could hear laughing and conversation coming from both inside and outside.

The place was full of life. Someone had brought a pair of big speakers out to the porch and hip hop blasted so loudly it shook the old boards. Girls laughed in groups near the coolers, and people danced barefoot under the stars. Beer cans littered the grass like confetti. Trevor stood there for a moment, taking it all in.

The moment was supposed to be his goodbye, but it felt like more than that. It felt like the whole town had come to see the end of one chapter and the beginning of another.

And then he noticed her.

Alyssa.

He had been aware of Alyssa for years, but he never allowed himself to express his feelings about her. She wasn't the loudest or flashiest girl in high school; but she was the one who was always on the go. Before the first bell, she had to go to varsity basketball practice. After class, she had to go to debate team practice. She also had to fit study groups into her already busy schedule. He used to sit in the back of Mr. Dawson's history class and tap a pencil against his desk as he watched her answer questions like she had the textbook memorized.

They had talked, yes, about little things. A smile when they worked jointly on a project and a quick "thanks" when he opened the door for her. But Trevor was the kind of guy who only hung out with his friends. He played football, worked part-time at a café, and spent weekends at the river drinking too much beer and not thinking enough. He admired her drive from afar, always thinking she was too good for him.

Up until the night of the party.

Tonight was supposed to be about loud music, coolers, and bonfires crackling on the sand, just like every other night. But Alyssa was here with a couple of friends, and for once, she didn't look like the girl who was always reading. She laughed a lot, and her hair was down instead of in its usual ponytail. Her eyes shone with firelight as she made fun of one of her friends for dancing off-beat. Trevor couldn't take his eyes off her. He couldn't stop telling himself that this might be his chance.

His friends saw it too. One of them nudged him with a smile. "Wow, she's right there. Talk to her, okay? What do you have to lose?"

Trevor thought of everything. His pride, his chance, and the delicate picture he had made of himself.

Even though he had a knot in his stomach, he made it across the crowded yard.

"Hey," he said, trying to sound casual. But his voice gave away his nerves. "What do you think of the party?"

She shrugged a little and didn't look at him much. "I guess it's fine."

Trevor's stomach dropped. Good job, genius. Before she leaves, give it another shot.

"Want to dance?" he asked, making himself smile.

"Not right now."

He gulped hard. Two strikes. Laughter and music went on around them as if the universe hadn't noticed his awkward attempts. "Want to get some air?" His voice sounded desperate. "It's quieter down by the river."

This time, she thought about it for a second before nodding. "Of course."

They slipped away from the noise, weaving between parked trucks and scattered lawn chairs until the trees swallowed them in shade. The river whispered beyond the clearing, and the night sky was expansive and full of stars. Alyssa's posture relaxed when she was away from the noise.

They began to talk, their words finding rhythm with each step. She told him about her plans for SIUE in the fall. She wanted to study education and one day teach middle school. Trevor admired and envied the sure way she spoke about her future. She had a direction.

"How about you?" She looked at him in the dark.

Trevor was unsure. It felt too heavy to tell her the truth: that he was lost, broke, and holding onto a choice he hadn't told her about yet. He smoothed out the edges. "Community college is in the next town. At first, just generals."

Her face didn't change much, but he still saw it: the flicker of polite disinterest, the coolness he'd seen before with people she would rather not get close to. She didn't push for more information. Instead, the conversation moved to easier topics like jokes, school memories, and little laughs that came more easily as they walked.

Eventually, headlights shone through the trees, signaling her sister's arrival. Trevor knew Alyssa wasn't safe to drive because she had been drinking. He walked her to the car, and with each step, the knot in his chest got tighter. The moment was getting away. Should I kiss her? Should I ask her out? Both?

He blurted it out before he had a chance to reconsider "Do you want to go out to dinner and see a movie sometime?"

She turned around and smiled softly, and her eyes were warmer than they had been all night. "Yes. That sounds good."

Trevor's heart raced. "Great. I'll pick you up next Saturday at five."

"Sounds like a date." She smiled and got into the passenger seat.

Trevor watched the red taillights move through the trees until they disappeared around the bend. The night was full of crickets and the sound of laughter from the party fading away. Trevor stayed where he was. He smiled, and then did a silly little victory dance, making sure no one could see it in the dark.

This was it, the start of something.

That night, Trevor walked home with his hands deep in his pockets, the gravel crunching under his boots. He felt the weight of the day with every step, and his mind going in circles, examining every detail, every word he had said, and every look Alyssa had given him. He kept looking for a mistake he might have made, but he couldn't find one. When he finally lay down in bed, sleep wouldn't come. His body needed to rest, but his nerves were buzzing like power lines in a storm. He stared at the ceiling for hours until he was so worn out sleep finally came.

# CHAPTER TWO

*T*he next morning, the recruiting office smelled like old coffee and floor wax. Trevor talked to the small group of men who would be going with him to MEPS. Grant rounded them up into a half-circle and spoke in a sharp, commanding voice.

"Everyone will meet here tomorrow. We'll spend the night at the hotel in St. Louis. No tricks. We'll be keeping an eye on you."

Trevor smiled to himself. Some of the guys had hoped for a wild send-off, but that didn't happen.

He tried to get to know the other recruits, but Grant stopped him and pulled him aside. "Watch Johnson," he told them. "He likes to smoke weed and drink. It's your job to make sure he passes."

Trevor blinked. "Yes, Sergeant. No problem." His voice was steady and sure. But on the inside, anger was building. Why do I have to watch the kids? That's his life, not mine. Even so, Grant's tone made him think this was more than just a casual job. It could be a test to see if Trevor knew that the Army wasn't about him. It was all about the group.

That night, Trevor worked at the Lake Front Café,

flipping burgers while grease popped on his forearms and the sound of the fryer was loud in his ears. Customers complained about everything and nothing, like cold fries and slow orders. Trevor swallowed his anger and thought, "I can't wait for this to be over. This place. This life."

His bag was ready by morning. He went back to the recruiting office where the group had grown so much that it could fit in three passenger vans. The air was thick with nervous silence. People didn't say much. Everyone was stuck in their own heads.

Trevor found out that Johnson would be his roommate when they got to the hotel. Well, damn. Let's get started.

Johnson wasn't as wild as Grant said he was, which surprised him. They talked about sports, music, and trucks. Later, the recruits met in the hotel dining room where the sound of silverware clattering and people talking filled the air. People from all branches of the military mixed collectively, and strangers shared the same nervous energy. Trevor went around and talked to people, even though he didn't want to. It was like being back in high school, with everyone posing, sizing each other up, and waiting for the next move.

People spread rumors quickly when a Marine recruit asked guys to come up to her room. There was no mistaking Johnson's smile. "I'm looking into it."

He came back two hours later, shaking his head in disbelief. "She was taking turns with different men," he said, sounding both shocked and amused. People in the group were disgusted, and some even laughed, but Johnson just shrugged, as if it were just another story to tell later.

Trevor knew Johnson hadn't touched any drugs or alcohol. Nothing Grant warned him about had come true.

They went upstairs early, knowing reveille would come soon. Trevor fell asleep on the hard mattress, but it didn't last.

The door shook with a loud pounding.

"Downstairs! Now!"

He squinted at the clock's bright red numbers. 0400. His heart raced. Wow.

He quickly put on his clothes, grabbed his bag, and ran down the hall with the others.

The vans drove through the dark morning, their headlights cutting through the road. This time, the quiet wasn't nerves. It was fatigue.

As soon as Trevor got out of the van at MEPS he stretched his stiff legs, but he was immediately yelled at.

"Shut up and get in line!" a Marine yelled, his voice cutting through the air like a whip.

Trevor stopped stretching and his body started moving toward the line before his mind did. The processing center was a mess, with hundreds of recruits crammed in from wall to wall, shuffling forward like cows.

Paperwork. More forms to fill out. A series of tests that never seemed to end. They took blood, checked vision, and measured hearing. It turned into one long line of waiting rooms and orders yelled by men in uniform.

The worst part came next when they were ordered to take off their clothes in a cold room. Marines yelled orders that echoed off the walls. "Get down! Stretch! Move!" The embarrassment was clear as a hundred bodies moved awkwardly while men with clipboards watched. Everyone laughed at an overweight recruit when a Marine said, "Goddamn, son, lay off the cookies."

When they started the urine test, the laughter stopped right away. Trevor drank so much water his stomach sloshed as he stood in line with the others. He finally got to go to the bathroom when it was his turn. A Marine was right behind him, watching every move he made.

A Coast Guard recruit next to him fidgeted and froze. He had been standing there for minutes, unable to move.

"Boy, piss! Get out of here!" the Marine yelled.

The recruit snapped back with a shaky voice, "I can't when you're yelling at me."

The Marine's face got darker. "If I don't get your piss in three minutes, I'll squeeze it out of you like an orange!"

Trevor almost laughed, but he stopped when the Marine's eyes turned sharply to him. "Do you think that's funny?"

"No, Sergeant," Trevor said under his breath, staring straight at the wall until he finally filled the cup. He quickly gave it to the Marine and rushed back into line.

Hours dragged by. At last, the processing was done and they were led into a room where they raised their right hands and took the oath. The words made Trevor feel both proud and relieved. This wasn't a touchdown in high school or applause from the stands. This was heavier, longer-lasting, and a promise to something bigger than him.

Trevor signed the last of the enlistment papers, the black ink sinking into the neat lines of military forms. Near the bottom of the contract, the details stood out: a six-year service commitment and a sign-on bonus of $20,000. He paused, letting the number sink in. That money would clear his debts and give him a clean slate, but the weight of six years in uniform pressed against the back of his mind.

Trevor let out a long breath. This is it. This is real. I made the right decision.

Staff Sergeant Grant gave him a pat on the back. "Good job. I hope you enjoy Kentucky. You're going to Fort Knox."

Trevor's heart raced. "When do I leave?"

"Come by tomorrow," Grant said. "I'll have the details."

The next morning the smell of coffee and copier toner filled the recruiting office. Grant stood behind his desk flipping through a thin manila folder. He handed it to Trevor.

"Second week of August," Grant said without any emotion. "In two months. You and your partner will go to

Fort Knox for basic and AIT. Twenty-two weeks."

Trevor's eyes were drawn to the number. Twenty-two weeks. Almost six months. Not a chance. His stomach dropped. He had known it would take a long time, but seeing it in print made the promise feel like an anchor dropped at his feet. He left the office holding the orders as if they might burn his hand. Doubt nagged at the edges of his mind as he walked to his truck. Could he really do it? Twenty-two weeks away from home and everything he knew?

But he quickly pushed the thought away. No more greasy aprons. No standing over fryers or angry customers. He didn't have to wonder what he was going to do with his life anymore. Just keep going. Move forward. He finally felt like he had a direction and something solid to stand on after years of feeling lost.

# CHAPTER THREE

*T*revor woke up with a tight ball of nervous energy in his stomach. Then he remembered. Tonight was the night. His first date with Alyssa. He sat up, rubbed his face, and said, "Well, great. Before she sees it, I need to clean up that truck. I don't want her to think I'm a slob."

As he pulled out a bucket and a rag, the morning sun shone on the driveway. He crouched down by the tires and scrubbed off the dried mud. Then he moved up to the hood and polished the faded paint until it almost shone.

His dad came out of the garage with a coffee cup in his hand. He leaned against the doorframe and watched with a half-smile that meant he was amused. "What is this about? Are you running for mayor or something?"

Trevor looked up and smiled shyly. "Nope. Cleaning the truck for my date tonight."

His dad raised an eyebrow. "With whom?"

"Alyssa."

His dad blinked for a second, then let out a low whistle. "Well, I'll be damned. That's good. You need to let me know how it goes."

Trevor nodded and pulled on the rag in his hand. "I hope it goes well. I really like this girl.'

The look on his dad's face changed and the smile turned into something more serious. "Have you told her yet that you're going into the Army?"

Trevor stiffened, and his rag stopped in the middle of a swipe. "Not yet. But I will."

His dad shook his head slowly and stared into his coffee, as if the steam held the truth about what would happen next. "You should. She has a right to know."

Trevor shrugged quickly, trying to sound casual even though his chest was getting tight. "I know. I'll let her know."

By the time the truck's tires were shiny, the dashboard was clean, and a fresh pine tree air freshener hung from the mirror, Trevor pictured her climbing in and noticing the shine. She always teased her sister about her messy car, so he figured she'd appreciate the difference. That thought gave him hope it might be enough to impress her.

That afternoon, he and his friends met up for lunch at the burger place in the next town over. The cracked leather booths, greasy smell, and buzzing neon sign over the counter hadn't changed in years. They got out of their trucks and went into the building where they started joking around before the waitress even brought them menus.

The usual food was burgers, fries, and shakes. And as

soon as they got there, the questions began.

"So," one friend asked, leaning over the table, "did you sign?"

Trevor nodded and put a fry in his mouth. "I did. Kentucky boot camp. Fort Knox. Two months from now."

Everyone around the table cheered. "Oh snap, dude! That's a lot. Happy for you," another said, patting him on the back.

Then someone smiled. "And the date tonight?"

Trevor couldn't help but grin. "I'm taking her to a nice restaurant and then to a movie near the city."

"Wow, pulling out all the stops," one person teased, raising his eyebrows. "Are you trying to get something?"

Trevor shook his head and smiled even though he didn't want to. "Nope. I just want to impress her. She's really great."

They all looked at him like he'd grown horns.

He let out a nervous laugh. "What?"

One of them crossed his arms and leaned back. "Man, you're leaving in two months. What do you think she will do about that?"

Trevor paused and ran his finger through a ring of condensation on the table. "I'm not sure. I'm going to tell her... but I'm waiting. Don't say anything."

His friend said, "No worries," and raised his hand as if to

swear an oath.

The talk turned to parties on the weekend, who was dating whom, and a new set of speakers someone had. When they left, the sun was getting lower in the sky and Trevor's nerves came back full force. It wasn't just dinner and a movie; it felt like the start of something, and he wasn't sure if that something would be able to handle what was coming next.

Trevor stood in front of the bathroom mirror at home, holding a comb in one hand and gel in the other, trying to get his thick black hair to behave. He frowned, tilted his head, smoothed a strand, and tried again. His mother's angry voice came from the hallway.

"Trevor, you've been in there a long time! You know other people live in this house, right?"

He ignored her and stared at his reflection as if it held the answer to his whole night. Okay, this is it. He opened his closet and looked at the rows of shirts as if he were getting ready for a pageant. He finally chose a pair of jeans and a yellow polo that looked good against them and also showed off the dark waves of his hair. Respectful, clean, and simple. He put a little cologne on his neck and breathed out.

His stomach was already in knots when he got into his freshly polished truck. On the way to Alyssa's house, he practiced his lines by tossing them around in his head. Each one sounded awkward and wrong. He finally gave up and said, "Screw it. I just need to be me."

Trevor wiped his hands on his jeans before ringing the doorbell. The chime echoed softly inside, and then there were muffled footsteps. When the door opened, he saw a stern-looking man standing in the doorway like a wall.

Alyssa's dad, Mark. With his arms crossed over his chest and his shoulders broad and square, he looked ready for anything. His icy blue eyes, sharp as cut glass, quickly scanned Trevor from head to toe, like a soldier checking for danger.

"So," Mark said flatly, his voice carrying the weight of someone already informed. "You're Trevor, the one taking my daughter out tonight."

Trevor straightened his back, forcing his voice to stay steady. "Yes, sir."

It was hard to tell what Mark's grunt meant. Approval? A warning? He moved over just enough for Trevor to get by. "Come in, I guess."

The house smelled faintly of fresh coffee and lemon polish. It was the kind of clean, organized home Trevor had never lived in before. There were pictures of Alyssa in the hallway. One of her in a basketball uniform and one with her in a cap and gown from high school. There was also one of her parents standing behind her on vacation, proud and protective. Each frame was like a silent reminder that she belonged in this world and that he was still trying to prove he should be able to enter it.

Linda, Alyssa's mom, got up from the couch in the living room. She smiled warmly, but it didn't show in her eyes. She wore a simple cardigan over a floral blouse, and her hair was pulled back neatly. Every detail was neat and well-planned. Trevor felt uneasy, thinking she could learn more about him in five seconds than he could in an hour of reading about her.

"So, Trevor." She motioned for him to sit down, but the way she spoke made it clear this was an interview, not a greeting. "Where do you work?"

Trevor sat on the edge of the armchair with his hands clasped tightly. "Part-time at a café by the lake, ma'am. I've been there a little over a year."

Linda nodded once, her face unreadable, and then she quickly asked, "And what are your plans? What's next?"

He swallowed. There it was: the question he didn't want to answer, the one that felt like the heaviest weight he had ever lifted at the gym. He cleared his throat. "I'm going to community college for now. I'm just getting my general education out of the way."

Linda tilted her head to the side a little. She wasn't being rude, but she also wasn't sure about him. Before Trevor could get back on his feet, another question came up.

"Do you go to church?" she asked.

Trevor thought for a second. "Not all the time, ma'am. But I grew up with it. My grandma made sure of that." He tried to smile a little, hoping it didn't look forced.

Linda and Mark looked at each other. Mark was standing in the doorway with his arms crossed like a guard. Trevor saw the flash of doubt that passed between them.

He kept saying to himself, "God, please let Alyssa hurry."

Then she came down the stairs wearing a pale sundress that swayed around her knees. Her blonde hair caught the light in soft waves. Trevor's breath hitched and everything else faded away. Whoa.

She asked, "Are you ready?" Her voice was light, but her smile was mischievous, as if she knew how he felt.

"Yeah," Trevor said, almost too quickly.

He heard her dad's voice, and it brought him back. "Bring her home on time."

"Yes, sir," Trevor said, already opening the door for Alyssa.

When they were outside, she rolled her eyes. "I'm sorry about my parents. They can be... a lot."

Trevor smiled. "It's all good. It makes the night more fun."

"So," she asked as they got to the truck, "what's the plan?"

"Movie and dinner close to the city."

"Perfect."

The drive went by quickly, with lots of laughing and talking. Trevor noticed how clean and sweet her perfume smelled, like vanilla, and how real her laughter sounded when she teased him.

They slid into a booth at the restaurant and ordered. It was like the conversation had been waiting years to be spoken. They talked about teachers they didn't like, their hopes for the future, and what they would do after high school. Trevor didn't feel like he had to perform this time, but he still avoided talking about the Army.

He was so mesmerized by her that by dessert, he couldn't look away.

"Are you okay?" she asked, tilting her head.

"Yes," he said, turning red. "I was just... lost in your beautiful blue eyes."

Alyssa's cheeks turned pink and she laughed softly.

Trevor bought popcorn and two sodas at the theater, feeling nervous because he hoped she would like the comedy he had chosen. Halfway through, he had the guts to put his arm around her shoulders. For a second, he was afraid she would move away, but instead, she leaned in and rested her head against him. A warm feeling spread through his chest. He thought he had won, but he fought back a grin.

On the drive back, she put her fingers through his, and the truck cab seemed to be full of quiet electricity. A group of Trevor's friends in a grocery store parking lot waved them down as they drove through town.

They yelled, "Are you going to the party tonight?"

"Of course," Alyssa said. "We have time."

At the party, Twista was coming out of the speakers. Loud and full of hip-hop beats and bass that shook the windows.

Trevor awkwardly talked to people inside until Alyssa pulled him over to her friends. They asked him a lot of questions about college, work, and whether or not he liked their girl. Trevor tried to be charming, but he could tell they were judging him behind smiles.

Later, Alyssa pulled him into the woods with a giggle. Trevor held her face in his hands and kissed her in the shadows of the trees with fireflies blinking all around. First softly, then more deeply.

Alyssa stayed close after they broke up, her lips brushing against his as she said, "I'm having such a great time tonight."

Trevor laughed without taking a breath, and his smile grew wider. "Me too. I really don't want it to end."

They walked back to the party with smiles on their faces they couldn't hide, then stayed just long enough to say goodbye before leaving.

They kissed in the truck as if they had been waiting for years. Alyssa leaned in closer and put her hand on his arm. There were a lot of laughs and easy silences on the way back to her house.

Trevor tried to say something in her driveway, but Alyssa kissed him again to shut him up.

"Did you have a good night?" he asked when they finally pulled back and walked to her door.

"Of course," she said, and her smile lit brighter than the porch light above her.

He said, "I'll pick you up Tuesday."

"Come over for dinner," she said.

"Okay. It's a date."

Trevor drove off with his heart racing and a big smile on his face. He had been through every moment of the evening a dozen times by the time he crawled into bed. When he finally fell asleep, he couldn't stop thinking about Alyssa's smile.

## CHAPTER FOUR

*I*t was three long days before Tuesday came and he could finally pull into Alyssa's driveway for their second date. His stomach was tied up in knots from both nerves and excitement. Tonight wasn't just about Alyssa. Tonight meant sitting across the dinner table from her parents, answering their questions, and proving himself worthy. It felt like a different kind of test, one that might be harder than any he would take in uniform.

As Trevor climbed the steps and rang the doorbell, the porch light made the siding look soft. His heart beat loudly in his ears. The door creaked open a moment later and Alyssa's mom came out. Her smile was warm and practiced, but the way she looked at him made his palms sweat.

"Come in, Trevor," she told him. "We have a special surprise for you tonight. I made my famous lasagna."

Trevor's face lit up with real relief. "That sounds great. I really like lasagna."

"Great!" Linda moved to the side and pointed him in. "Why don't you sit down while Alyssa and I finish putting the table together?"

The house smelled like comfort, with garlic, baked cheese,

and something that smelled like flowers. Maybe a candle. Trevor sat down on the couch, still a little stiff. Alyssa's dad sat in his recliner watching a baseball game on TV. He didn't stand up or smile; he just nodded at Trevor and turned back to the screen.

"Are you a fan of the Cardinals?" Trevor asked, trying to sound relaxed.

Mark grunted and didn't look away. "Is there any other team?"

Trevor made himself laugh. "Not sure."

He shifted uncomfortably in his seat in the silence that followed and was glad when Alyssa came in a moment later with her hair down. She wore a quiet smile.

There was a bowl of crisp salad, golden lasagna, and garlic bread that shone with butter. Trevor sat across from Alyssa, and her knee brushed against his under the table, which helped him stay grounded. The talk started off light: school, his part-time job at the café, and his family. He was honest with his answers, but they were short so he wouldn't give away what he was really planning.

Linda's questions had an edge to them; they were polite but curious. "So, Trevor," she asked between bites, "are you looking forward to starting school this fall?"

Trevor hesitated and stabbed his fork into the lettuce on his plate. "Yes, ma'am. I am. I think community college is the right place to start and get my generals done, then I'll see where it leads."

Linda hummed as if she wasn't sure what to think. Mark finally looked up, his eyes sharp, and looked at Trevor like he was a batter at the plate. "Um." It wasn't a word of approval; it was just a placeholder.

Alyssa's hand slipped into Trevor's under the table. He held on, thankful, but the knot in his stomach didn't go away.

The mood got a little better by dessert. Linda brought out pie, and Trevor was able to laugh at Alyssa's jokes, which helped him feel better.

Linda then pulled out a deck of cards. "Do you know how to play cards?"

Trevor shook his head. "Not really. But I can learn."

"Good," she said, already moving. "Best way to meet someone."

They played three hands. Trevor lost all of them. Alyssa teased him with a smug smile, and even though he had failed, he couldn't help but laugh. Even Mark smiled once. It wasn't quite approval, but it wasn't nothing, either.

Later, when Alyssa told her parents they were going into town, they looked at each other across the table. Not angry or rude, just careful, as if they weren't sure what to think of him yet. Linda gave the usual reminder to come back at a reasonable hour.

Trevor stood up and thanked her for dinner with a polite nod. Then he met Mark's eyes and shook the man's hand as firmly as he could. "It was great meeting you, sir." Mark's grip was steady and hard to read as he said, "Be careful on the road."

Alyssa put her hand back in his outside in the cool night air, and Trevor let out the breath he had been holding for hours.

As soon as they got into his truck, Alyssa leaned in closer. "Stop ahead."

He parked in the lot behind the community center and barely turned off the engine before she pulled him in for a kiss. It was both sweet and hungry, the kind that made everything else fade away. It was warm against his cheek when she finally pulled away.

"Thank you for eating with my family tonight," she said quietly. "I think it went well."

Trevor smiled. "Anytime. I'm learning how to play spades."

She teased, "Is that why you lost every game?"

"Maybe I was distracted," he said, looking at her.

She smiled, and they both laughed.

The night took them to the park by the lake, where music played from open car doors and streetlights buzzed like tired fireflies. They talked to their friends for a while, but then Alyssa gave him a look that said, "Let's go." He didn't think twice.

He asked, "Do you want to drive around to the other side of the lake?"

She nodded like she knew what was going on. Everyone in town knew that place.

He put in a new CD with slow R&B ballads and a few Usher songs. Soon they were tangled up in the shadows, and the heat was rising fast. Trevor was shocked to see how far they had gone. Just as they were getting their bearings, a loud knock on the window made them jump.

A police officer from the city stood outside shining a light inside that bounced off the glass.

Trevor rolled the window down halfway. "Yes, officer?"

The cop said, "You kids need to move along."

"Yes, sir." Trevor nodded quickly.

The officer walked back to his cruiser, and as soon as his taillights went out, Trevor and Alyssa burst out laughing, their hearts still racing.

They drove around town for a while, wasting time in the best way they knew how, laughing at each other's jokes, letting the music spill from the speakers, and pretending the night could stretch on forever. Trevor kept one eye on the clock, knowing he'd have to take her home soon, but for now, he just wanted the drive to last.

The porch light was on when he pulled into Alyssa's driveway. Mark stood there with his arms crossed and his brow furrowed, waiting. Trevor felt the usual nerves and respect that came whenever he faced him.

Alyssa turned to her dad, her cheeks red. "Hey, Dad."

Mark's look at Trevor was sharp, but not mean. "You're out late again, huh?"

Trevor nodded steadily. "We lost track of time a little, but I managed to get her home safely. I hope that's okay?"

Mark's eyes stayed on Trevor for a long moment, then he gave a short nod.

Alyssa leaned in and kissed him quickly on the lips in the porch light. It was soft and warm. "Have a good night's sleep. Dream about me," she said softly.

Trevor smiled, and his chest felt tight with happiness. "Only if you do the same," he said.

He straightened up and looked at Mark again. This time, Mark slowly nodded. The caution was still there, but Trevor hoped he was starting to like him. His eyes swung to Alyssa. "See you on Friday?" Trevor asked.

"Sounds good," Alyssa said. She brushed his hand as she walked toward the door.

"I'll pick you up just before lunch," he said.

"Perfect," she said with a smile.

Trevor looked at Mark for a moment and gave him a small, respectful nod before getting into his truck. Even though he knew it would take time to get Mark's full approval, he felt a connection with him that made him want to prove himself—not just as Alyssa's boyfriend, but as someone her dad could trust.

Trevor felt lighter and stronger as he drove home through

the quiet night. For once, the world seemed to be going his way. He was so excited for Friday.

# CHAPTER FIVE

*T*revor worked for three long days that got worse with each sunrise. He flipped burgers at Lake Front Cafe under the harsh fluorescent lights and counted down the hours until he could call Alyssa. He finally spoke to her that night, his voice shaky and full of hope. "Do you want to come to my house around lunch tomorrow?"

Alyssa laughed. "Of course. I'll be there around noon."

Trevor's nerves were buzzing like electricity through his veins the next day. He looked through the blinds when he heard a car pull into the driveway. There she was, getting out of her car like the sun had turned into a person. He ran outside with his heart racing.

Alyssa hugged him tightly and he picked her up off the ground for a short, dizzying moment before putting her back on solid ground. Their laughter mixed and flowed across the driveway like music.

He took her around the property, pointing out the little things he thought were important: his parents' garage, the wall of tools he used to fix his truck, and how he had spent hours fixing engines. Alyssa didn't look very impressed, but her smile never faded and her eyes followed him, warm and curious.

Finally he stopped and said, "Want to head out of town and get some lunch at that burger place?" He tried to sound casual.

"Of course," she said, and the way her eyes lit up made his chest tighten.

The diner smelled like fried onions, fries, and soda. Alyssa surprised him by ordering the same thing he did: a burger, fries, and a cherry shake. They slid into a booth in the corner with plates of hot, steaming food. Trevor realized he could breathe as she ate, relaxed, and happy. She made him feel at ease, and that comforted him in ways that nothing else could.

After that, they walked through the park nearby, holding hands. Butterflies flew between flowers, and the sun shone on the paths. Trevor was amazed at how simple and perfect everything seemed.

"Look at the swings!" Alyssa's smile went from ear to ear. "Come swing with me."

Trevor laughed. "How old are we, ten?"

"Ten, I guess," she said with a smile as she jumped on a swing.

He went with her anyway, and for a while, they flew back and forth, kicking their legs high and laughing at each other. The world became smaller and smaller until it was just the two of them.

Trevor looked at the clock when he got back in the truck. They still had hours to go. "Do you want to drive to the city and see the butterfly house?" he asked.

She smiled. "That sounds great."

The highway went on and on, and the music in the cab filled the air. The sun shone on the dashboard. The butterfly house was even more magical than he had thought it would be when they got there. Thousands of wings brushed against them, soft and shiny. A monarch landed on Alyssa's shoulder, and Trevor couldn't stop looking at her beautiful smile.

"What?" she asked, noticing his gaze.

"Wow," he said. "Even the butterflies know how nice you are."

She leaned in for a soft kiss, and a blush came to her cheeks. The butterfly rose up and flew into the warm air above.

When Trevor got home, he saw a note on the counter saying his mom and dad would be gone overnight. He was alone here with Alyssa. His mind screamed, "Yes!"

"What does that say?" she asked.

He smiled and said, "Just that we have the place to ourselves."

She tilted her head, and her face was hard to read. "Oh, okay."

He shrugged and walked to the kitchen. "I'll make dinner for us. Want to help?"

"Do you know how to cook?" she asked playfully.

"Yeah," he said. "Mom thought I'd never get married. She

taught me, but mostly so she wouldn't have to cook."

Alyssa laughed. "So, what's for dinner?"

"Grilled steak, garlic mashed potatoes, and banana pudding."

Her eyes got big. "That sounds amazing."

They boiled potatoes, season steaks, steal kisses, and have fun. Trevor mixed the garlic, cream, and cheese into the potatoes and breathed in the smell, thinking, "Damn, I'm good." Alyssa leaned over and took a deep breath, her eyes shining with approval.

She asked, "Did you already make the banana pudding?"

"Yes. It was cold last night. Wanted it to be ready for today."

Dinner was warm and slow. Alyssa ate with gusto and praised him with every bite. Trevor smiled and kissed her hand, feeling a quiet sense of pride grow in his chest. He then brushed his teeth, put in some gum, and put a VHS of *Risky Business* in the player.

"You've never seen this?" he asked in shock when she asked what it was about.

"Nope."

"Well, you're in for a treat."

But the movie didn't really matter. They spent more time on the couch with their hands roaming and their lips searching, lost in the moment.

Finally, Alyssa pulled back just enough to say, "I think you should show me where you sleep."

Trevor's heart rate doubled, hoping he was ready for what might happen. They barely made it to his room before clothes were all over the floor and the outside world disappeared.

Afterward, all Trevor could get out was a quiet, "Wow."

Alyssa purred softly, and he smiled, thinking how great it had been. He looked at her face for signs of regret, but all he saw was a happy, playful smile. They kissed again and then fell asleep in each other's arms.

Alyssa woke up hours later. "Oh no! We have to get up. "I have to go home."

They quickly got dressed and Trevor walked her to her car. He opened the door, kissed her deeply and said, "Tonight was great."

She laughed and turned red. "It really was."

She called out, "See you tomorrow?" as she rolled down her window.

"Of course," he said. "I'll surprise you with the time."

Trevor leaned against the door and watched her taillights disappear down the road. He could still taste her kiss and hear her laugh. His heart raced in his chest and he knew one thing for sure: this was just the start.

# CHAPTER SIX

July 2000

*T*revor had been dating Alyssa for two months, and every day with her was better than the last. He was beginning to think he might be in love, and he thought Alyssa might be too.

But the pressure in his chest wouldn't go away. He would be leaving for Kentucky in two weeks to start basic training. He was nervous about telling her because she didn't know yet.

What if she thought he was lying? What if she left?

Trevor still knew it wasn't right to keep it from her. No matter how hard it was to say, she deserved the truth. He promised himself that tomorrow. He'd tell her everything tomorrow.

He called her the next day and tried to remain calm. "Hey, can you come here? I have something important to tell you."

Her interest peaked through the line. "What is it about?"

He said, "I'd rather tell you in person."

"Okay," she said. "I'm on my way."

Trevor's stomach was in knots by the time her car pulled up the driveway. He met her at the car, gave her a hug, and kissed her quickly. When they walked in, Alyssa looked confused.

"Have a seat," he said as he sat down in the chair across from her. He looked for the right words, but none came.

Alyssa finally spoke up. "Okay? What's so important?"

He couldn't stop the words from coming out. "I joined the Army. In two weeks, I'll be leaving for basic training in Kentucky."

Alyssa stopped moving, her face showing both confusion and disbelief.

"Are you all right?" Trevor asked carefully.

She squinted her eyes. "How long have you known this?"

"Two months," he said.

She looked at him in shock. "So, you knew this whole time we were dating? Why didn't you tell me?"

He looked down. "I don't know. I didn't want to ruin the fun we were having."

"Well," she said coldly, "you just did."

Trevor sank deeper into his seat. "I'm sorry, Alyssa. I wanted to tell you so many times, but I couldn't find the right words. I didn't think I would fall in love with you either."

Alyssa's cheeks turned red. "You... love me?"

He stood up to get closer. "I do."

She turned away and her voice shook. "I love you too, but I need to think about this."

Alyssa ran to the door before Trevor could answer. He went outside after her, but she was already in the car with tears streaming down her face. He could only watch as her taillights faded into the night and a tear fell down his own cheek.

He thought, "I might have just ruined something great. What did I do? Could I have done it in a different way? I really messed that up."

The next few days went by very slowly. Trevor sat around the house staring at the phone, hoping she would call or at least answer when he did. Finally, he got a call.

"Is it okay if I come over?" Alyssa's voice was soft. "How about you make dinner?"

He felt a wave of relief. "Of course. What do you want?"

"Surprise me."

"Okay," Trevor said, and for the first time in days, he smiled. "Sounds like a date."

She even chuckled a little. "Talk to you soon."

Trevor ran to the store and then returned home to cooked dinner. Pork steaks, potato salad, and pie with coconut cream. He heard her car in the driveway while the steaks were cooking on the grill. She walked up to the deck and Trevor ran to hug her and kiss her lightly.

"How are you?"

"Good," she said.

"What?" he asked, seeing the strange look on her face. His stomach turned again and he thought, "Please don't go."

"Are you ready to eat?"

She nodded.

They sat outside and Trevor could see she had a lot of questions on her mind. "Go ahead," he said softly. "Ask me."

Alyssa was able to smile. "Why the army?"

He took a big breath. "To be honest? It's a great job with good benefits, and it gives me a reason to get up in the morning. I don't think I could handle college work right now, and there aren't many good jobs around here. "This seems like the right way to go."

She nodded slowly. "I understand. But how long are you going to be gone?"

"Basic and AIT together? Around twenty-two weeks."

Her eyes got bigger. "That's too long. I don't think I can handle that."

Trevor's shoulders drooped. "I get it. But we can send letters to each other, and when I get phone privileges, we can talk. It won't be easy, but it's something."

Alyssa let out a sigh. "That's okay, but it's not the same."

His head fell.

"Don't think I'm breaking up with you," she said quickly. "Because I love you."

Trevor's head jerked up. "You love me?"

She quietly said, "I do. And I'm mad you didn't tell me sooner, but I understand why."

He whispered, "Thank you."

"So, what's the next step?" he asked.

Alyssa stood up straight, her eyes steady. "We're going to make the most of these next two weeks. I'll be here when you leave and when you get back."

Trevor smiled with relief. "That works for me."

After dinner, he brought out the coconut cream pie. Alyssa poked at hers with a thoughtful look on her face.

"What's going on in your beautiful mind? What's up?" Trevor asked.

She blinked and came back to reality. "I'm sorry. I have a million thoughts going through my head. But I'll be fine."

"Don't be afraid to ask questions, Alyssa."

She nodded. "Okay, then. What will you do in the Army?"

Trevor smiled a little. "They call it a job, a MOS. "Cavalry Scout."

Alyssa tilted her head, interested. "So, what does a Cavalry Scout do, exactly?"

Trevor took a deep breath and tried to explain it in a way that didn't sound too serious. "Well, in a nutshell, we're the Army's eyes and ears. A scout's job is to go ahead of the main group and find out what's in the way of them getting to the enemy. Like enemy positions, the terrain, or anything else that could help or hurt. We sneak in, get information, and come back to tell others about it, usually before anyone else even gets close."

Alyssa frowned a little. "So... you guys are the first ones out there? That sounds like it could be dangerous."

"Yeah," Trevor said, forcing a smile. "It can be. We drive cars, walk sometimes, and need to be quick, quiet, and smart. We have to make sure the Army knows what they're getting into if they're about to move. Think of it like scouting ahead so that everyone else has a chance to win."

Her eyes softened, but she was still worried. "That sounds like a big deal. But also, scary."

Trevor shrugged, trying to keep things light. "It matters. And yes, it's a little scary. But I picked this job. I wanted to do something that was important."

Alyssa put her fork down and looked at him. Her eyes were soft but searching.

"Trevor, why do you want to do this? Why do you want to join the Army? Why do you want to do something that's important?"

Trevor leaned back in his chair and his chest got tight. He didn't answer for a long time, just stared out at the yard as if the words he needed were hiding in the grass. At last he let out a sigh.

"I don't want to be just another guy stuck in a dead-end job, hating every day. I want to show myself that I can do more than I am now. Alyssa, I want to stand for something. To do something that matters, not just for me, but for everyone who depends on us."

Alyssa's lips were pressed together. She seemed like she wanted to fight, but she also seemed to get it. When she spoke again, her voice shook. "That's nice, Trevor, but it's also what scares me the most."

As she listened, Alyssa's eyes filled with tears. She was quiet for a moment, then she reached across the table and touched his hand.

She said softly, "I understand now, but I don't like it. I hate the idea of you being in danger. But I understand why it matters to you. And if it matters to you, then I guess I can work on this. On us. On how to be okay with it."

Trevor squeezed her hand and felt better. "Do you mean that?"

She nodded a little. "I love you, Trevor. I know it won't be easy, but I'm willing to try if you are."

Trevor held her face in his hands. "I love you too. And I'm willing to give it a shot, Alyssa. You have no idea how much I appreciate your honesty."

They both got up at almost the same time and hugged each other tightly, as if the world outside didn't exist. Alyssa's shoulders shook as she cried, and Trevor felt her warm tears wet his shirt.

He kept saying, "It's going to be okay. I promise."

She nodded and kissed him through her tears, not able to find the words.

Later, they cuddled up in the living room with a movie playing in the background while Trevor's mind raced. He held her close, feeling both relieved and unsure, hoping she meant every word she had said.

Trevor walked Alyssa to her car when it was time for her to leave. He kissed her goodbye and then stood in the driveway watching her taillights fade into the darkness. He waited until they were completely gone before going back inside.

The next two weeks were nothing short of incredible. Trevor and Alyssa were with each other almost all the time. They went on dates, hung out with friends. When they were together, nothing else mattered. They laughed until their sides hurt, talked for hours, and held hands like they never wanted to let go.

They talked on the phone every night, their voices soft and full of laughter as they told each other secrets and rested in the quiet comfort of knowing that someone really cared. Their love for each other grew stronger, deeper, and more certain every day. By the end of the two weeks, it felt like they were the only two people in the world. The thought of being apart was almost too much to bear, but they made the most of every moment they had left.

The day before Trevor was to leave, his friends wanted to throw a party.

"Come on, man," one of them said. "It's going to be great!"

Trevor smiled. "Count me in."

He called Alyssa to tell her, and she said she would come.

They arrived at the same time, and were shocked by how many people were there. People they didn't even know had come, and the house and yard were full of laughter and conversation. People came up to Trevor to congratulate him on joining the Army, and Alyssa's friends asked her a lot of questions.

Trevor thought, "No way. This is strange, but fun."

There was a bonfire in the backyard, and music played in the night air. The flames shone in Alyssa's eyes, and Trevor felt a warm rush of happiness.

One of his friends came up to him. "So, I guess she handled it well?"

"Not at first. But she got it after we talked. It might be hard, especially at first, but I hope we can work it out."

His friends stared at him with wide eyes.

"What's going on? What did I say?"

One of them said, "We're just surprised that you never put this much effort into girls before."

Trevor smiled a little. "I love her."

One of the guys almost threw up his beer. "Are you kidding me?"

Trevor said firmly, "Nope. I love her."

Everyone was quiet for a moment before they all raised their bottles. They yelled and everyone chugged down the rest of their beer.

Trevor looked through the crowd for Alyssa. He hoped she was laughing and talking with her friends, probably about him. He walked up to her, took her hand, and asked, "How is everyone?"

Her friends looked at him with a mix of disbelief and fake anger.

One of them said, "I can't believe you can just walk away from her like that!"

Trevor smiled and moved closer to Alyssa. "I'm not doing this for myself alone. I'm doing it for her too." He kissed her softly, and all of her friends said, "Aww!"

There was music, dancing, and laughter all night long. They spent time with friends, told stories, and enjoyed every second they had. They drank too much, so they walked a few yards back to Trevor's house, holding hands tightly, ready to spend the night before the big day.

The world outside felt quiet and private. Trevor pulled Alyssa close, and they kissed deeply, staying in each other's arms for a long time. Their laughter and talking turned into soft touches and quiet words, and then the rest of the world was gone.

That night they made love, holding each other close and feeling their hearts beat in time with each other. They cherished the closeness and connection that had grown between them over the past two months. Afterward they lay with each other, wrapped in each other's arms, breathing softly, and enjoying the closeness words could never fully describe.

The next morning came too soon. When Trevor woke up, soft light was coming in through his bedroom window and Alyssa was still curled up against his chest. He held her there for a few precious moments, remembering how warm she was and how she breathed, knowing that soon everything would be different.

They all got in the car after a quick breakfast and drove to the recruiting office. Trevor's parents rode along in a car behind him, quiet but proud. A few of his closest friends followed in another car. Alyssa sat next to him, holding his hand and giving him strength without saying a word.

Trevor finished the last paperwork at the recruiting office. The forms that marked the start of a life he had only imagined made him realize how real it was that he was leaving. His parents hugged him tightly and said nice things to him. His friends patted him on the back with teasing smiles that barely hid how worried they were.

At last, it was time to head to the airport. Alyssa stayed close and wouldn't let go of his hand. "I'll write every day," she said quietly, her voice shaking.

Trevor said, "I'll write too. And call me whenever you can."

When they got to the gate, no one said anything for a long time. Trevor's heart was heavy because he loved Alyssa.

His parents hugged him again and their eyes were full of tears. His friends crowded around him, making last jokes and patting him on the back. But the hug from Alyssa meant the most. She put her head on his chest and whispered, "I love you. Come back to me."

"I will," Trevor said, kissing her on the head. "I love you too. More than anything."

Then he let go of her hand and walked toward the plane that would take him to Fort Knox. His heart was full, and the memories of their love burned brightly in his chest.

Trevor got on the plane and looked back one last time. Alyssa was at the gate, crying and waving until the plane's engine drowned out her voice.

He put his hand on his chest to remember how warm she was, how she laughed, and how she looked at him with love and trust. He promised silently, "I'll come back to you," and the words echoed in his heart.

The world got smaller as the plane took off, and reality set in. There was uncertainty, challenge, and change ahead. But one thing was still true: Alyssa, their love, and the bond they had built over the past few months. They would hold on to each other in spirit, if not in body, as this new chapter of their lives began.

Trevor closed his eyes and leaned back in his chair. The roar of the engines turned into a quiet determination. He would always have her with him, no matter what happened next. And one day he would come back home.

# CHAPTER SEVEN

August 2000, Fort Knox

*W*hen the plane landed in Louisville, Trevor got his things and stepped onto the tarmac with a mix of excitement and nerves. He walked to the USO station, where a few uniformed people asked him for his orders right away and started calling him "trainee." He was ready for the worst, and his stomach tightened.

Trevor saw his first drill sergeant while waiting in line. Just being there seemed to demand attention. The sergeant quickly started showing them how to stand, how to act, and how to move with purpose. Every command felt strict, urgent, and impossible to ignore.

Then they were told they only had two minutes to call their loved ones. Two minutes isn't enough time to reassure anyone, even themselves. Trevor went to the pay phone and called his parents first. "Mom, Dad... I did it. I love you."

They said, "Love you too," in calm but proud voices.

He only had a second to catch his breath before calling Alyssa. She answered right away, and he spoke quickly. "I did it! I love you. Sorry, I can't talk for long, only a minute."

She said, "Love you too, miss you already. Do great things."

"I will. Don't forget to send letters. Bye."

After that, they got on a bus with their bags in their laps and went to Fort Knox. As Trevor and the others rode in silence, the scenery outside the windows blurred by.

The process got more intense when they arrived. They got off the bus and lined up again to face drill sergeants who went over the rules for behavior, the rules for how to act like a soldier, and the rules for how to stand at attention, parade rest, and other unspoken rules of discipline. After that, they were led into a big classroom where they learned their platoon duties and filled out more required forms.

Next was the shake-down room, where all signs of illegal goods were taken. They got their military gear after following the sergeant again. Then there were buzz cuts. Trevor couldn't believe what he was seeing as his hair fell off. He was scared, confused, and weighed down by the changes. Everything was being taken away, piece by piece.

After getting their buzz cuts, they all stood in line like cows, waiting for their turn to get shots. Trevor's stomach knotted as he took a step forward, and with each passing second, the fear of the unknown grew stronger.

They were told to hold their backpacks over their heads. Trevor had a hard time with the bag. His muscles were burning, and he thought, "This bag is heavier than it looks."

The drill sergeants started to teach them how to line up for chow once they were finally settled. "Cadence chow formation!" they yelled. At the first meal, there was a lot of yelling and giving orders about how to grab a plate, line up, and move collectively. Trevor had expected yelling, but the level of it was shocking.

The barrage kept going while we ate. A voice yelled, "Eat faster, trainee!" Trevor's heart raced as he realized that in this world, every second counted and there was no time to waste.

When everyone was settled, the drill sergeants came back. Their boots hit the floor in a way that made everyone in the room stand up straight. "Trainees! Outside! Now! Wait in line!"

Trevor and the others left, still feeling awkward and unsure. They all noticed how similar they looked, with their buzz cuts, identical gear, and wide-eyed expressions. The sun was bright outside, the ground was hard, and the drill sergeants' voices cut through the field like knives.

"Get out of the way! Make two lines!" one yelled. "Get up!" Look ahead! "You're not here to make friends!"

As they moved into place, Trevor could see the faces around him more clearly. He looked at the name tags stitched onto their uniforms: Harris, Lopez, Daniels, and a dozen others, all new, all nervous, all green. It was comforting to know that no one had experience, so no one had an advantage. They were all unsure what to do.

The drill sergeants made them do simple drills for the next hour, like marching, standing at attention, and shouting answers. Every mistake was loudly corrected, and every pause was met with a sharp command. But even with all the yelling and orders, small interactions started to happen. A whispered joke between two trainees, a shared grimace after a shouted correction, and a brief nod of support.

Trevor couldn't help but smile a little when Daniels messed up a command and Harris said, "Welcome to hell," under his breath. There was some humor, but it didn't last long. Nerves and shared struggle were making small connections. Trevor could feel it as they marched back to the barracks. These people, all new and with the same buzz cuts, were slowly becoming a group. They weren't friends yet, but they weren't complete strangers either.

He thought again, "We'll get through this, one step at a time."

The first week was a nonstop blur of pain, fatigue, and yelling. Trevor's body hurt from all the drills, and his mind was always racing. Every day they faced a new challenge that pushed them to their limits.

And now it was time for the tear gas chamber. Just saying the word made all the trainees nervous. Trevor had heard terrible stories of burning eyes, uncontrollable coughing, and panic, but the truth was even scarier: no one had ever been through this before. All of the trainees in the room were brand new.

They were put in a small, clean building. The drill sergeant's voice cut through the tension like a knife: "Trainees! Take off your masks! All at once! Now, tell me your full name and rank!"

The words were still there. Trevor's stomach was in knots.

All of us... at the same time? He glanced around. The other trainees, who were just as new as he was, were staring at him with wide eyes. Hands shook on the edges of the masks. People in the room started to panic.

They all took off their masks at the same time they were told to. The sharp sting hit right away, making eyes burn, noses smart, and generating coughs that made it hard to breathe. The sound of hacking and gasping drowned out the drill sergeant's voice. Trevor's lungs were screaming for air, and he was having trouble breathing.

But he made himself pay attention and shouted out his full name and rank. His voice broke, but he kept going, doing what they had told him to do. Everyone else around him was doing the same thing, though some were more clear than others. They were all new to this and didn't know exactly what they were doing.

It felt like every second lasted forever. The gas hurt their eyes, lungs, and throats. Panic was about to take over, but somehow, in the middle of all the chaos, they were all making it through. The fear of every trainee was the same as his. Every cough and gasp was a fight for both of them.

The drill sergeant yelled another command after about four minutes. "Out! Get out! Flap your arms like a bird as you go!"

Trevor blinked through the tears and then immediately started to comply, flapping his arms in an awkward way while coughing and stumbling toward the door. Around him, other trainees flailed in unison. Some laughed through their pain, while others were too shocked to do anything but move. It was embarrassing, tiring, and oddly unifying.

Trevor stumbled out into the fresh air, coughing and gasping for breath. Harris leaned against the wall, holding his mask with a nervous smile. "Well, that was bad."

Trevor laughed hoarsely, still trying to catch his breath. "Yeah, none of us have ever been through that before. We made it through it..."

For the first time that week, Trevor felt a spark of connection with the other people. They were all new, scared, and learning the hard way, but somehow, they were getting through it as one.

## CHAPTER EIGHT

August 2000, Fort Knox

*T*he second week hit like a hammer. Every morning, they followed the same strict schedule, but today was different: he had to do the confidence obstacle course. He stood at the starting line, squinting against the sun reflecting off the dusty ground. He couldn't help but think that this was harder than anything they ever did in football.

The first station was very hard. They crawled under low ropes, getting mud got all over their hands and knees. Trevor's chest hurt and his arms screamed, but he pushed himself to go on. "Come on, Trevor!" a teammate's voice rang out every time he thought he might slow down. "You can do this!"

He was sweating and had grit in every part of his uniform by the time he got to the wall climb. He realized it wasn't just about finishing; it was about everyone finishing. No one in the platoon could move on until every trainee finished all the stations. They weren't just trying to beat each other; they were trying to beat the whole group.

But the desire to compete didn't go away. Everyone wanted to be in first place. Trevor stumbled over the last wall, muddy and tired, and felt a rush of pride as the platoon cheered. The friendship that came from going through hard times was electric.

Next was the Victory Tower, a vertical nightmare of platforms and ropes that tested balance, courage, and trust. If someone made a mistake, they would fall, and each trainee relied on the others to see them, steady them, and cheer them on. Trevor gritted his teeth and climbed the tower, feeling every ache and pain from the week before. But he was still going.

They also learned how to fight with their hands, which made Trevor's shoulders hurt and his mind race. The drill sergeants never stopped correcting their posture, movements, and hesitations. Trevor couldn't stop thinking about how different this was from football. In this sport, every move could mean the difference between winning and losing.

Then came first-aid exercises that were like injuries on the battlefield. Trevor learned how to check for wounds, bandage them, and keep them stable while under a lot of stress, with the sun beating down on him and sweat stinging his eyes. Every job required concentration, endurance, and accuracy.

Finally, reading a map was a whole new challenge for them. They followed coordinates, learned how to use a compass, and navigated small courses while the drill sergeants watched. Trevor's mind was tired from all the physical work, and it was hard for him to keep up with the mental challenges, but he kept going, refusing to fall behind.

They were dirty, tired, and sunburned by the end of the day. Trevor's body hurt in ways he never thought was possible, but he smiled as the platoon got together. Harris smiled back and said, "Good work today. We did it."

Trevor nodded, breathing heavily. He was happy to have made it through another day and another test. Week Two was hard, but it taught him something very important: how to work with others, how to keep going, and how to never give up.

He thought, "One station at a time, one obstacle, one climb, one battle..."

Every Sunday they got a small, valuable reward: thirty minutes to talk to their loved ones. Trevor was more excited about it than anything else that week. But there was a catch: those thirty minutes weren't guaranteed; they had to be earned. The drill sergeants made it clear that the platoon had to behave, follow orders, and do everything perfectly all week. One mistake, one missed order, or one sign of laziness could cancel the reward.

When the order finally came, "Platoon, make your calls! The trainees lined up at the row of pay phones against the wall of the barracks. They all paid for their calls with calling cards, which they slid into the slots. While they waited, they balanced their gear by adjusting the cords.

Trevor picked up the phone and called his parents. Hearing the familiar voices on the other end was comforting. He spent about ten minutes going over everything he had done that week, including the drills, the obstacle courses, the confidence challenges, the first-aid training, and even the tear gas chamber. He could hear the pride in his parents' voices, which made the pain and tiredness feel a little better.

As soon as he hung up, he called Alyssa. They had the last twenty minutes to themselves. He told her how much he loved and missed her, and asked how school was going. He told her about the little wins and losses he'd had and tried to make her feel better by saying that he was doing well. Alyssa's voice was warm and supportive, and the connection reminded him of everything he was fighting for.

The thirty minutes felt like only seconds had gone by. Trevor didn't want to hang up when the drill sergeant yelled at him to do so. The barracks was quiet again, and the familiar hum of tiredness and getting ready for the next week took over.

It wasn't much, but in that short half-hour, Trevor felt a connection to the life he had left behind. It reminded him that boot camp took everything from him, but it didn't take away the people who mattered most. Earning that call week after week was worth it. No matter what it took.

The official start of Red Phase was Week Three. This was when the drill sergeants pushed them harder, faster, and closer to the edge than ever before. Trevor woke up again before the sun, his muscles sore from the week before, but he knew he couldn't rest. Every drill, every movement, and every command this week felt more important than ever.

Getting to know their assigned weapon, the M16A2 assault rifle, was the first big thing they had to do. Trevor's hands shook a little as he picked it up for the first time. He could feel the weight of the rifle and the cold metal against his palms. The voice of the drill sergeant was sharp. "Every time you move that weapon, you could save your life. Learn it. Be respectful of it. Master it."

They practiced loading, aiming, and firing every day, going over the same drills until the movements became second nature. Trevor's body hurt, but his mind got sharper. Every time you pulled the trigger, made an adjustment, or changed your stance, you had to pay attention. He was learning that discipline wasn't just about doing what you were told; it was also about being precise, being aware, and being on time.

Along with learning how to use weapons, the platoon practiced basic soldier skills. Hand-to-hand combat drills tested their strength, speed, and reaction time. Life-saving drills forced them to think clearly under pressure while they bandaged wounds, did CPR, and helped a fake casualty. Trevor's muscles hurt from working out, but the knowledge felt important and gave him a sense of purpose.

By noon, they were ready to put all the lessons to the test in their first field exercise, The Hammer. Just the name made hearts race. The platoon moved at the same time through a fake battlefield, putting the skills they had learned under stress to use. Trevor crawled through mud, moved with his M16A2, and stabilized "wounded" teammates, all while following orders and keeping up with the group. The drill sergeants quickly fixed every mistake and gave a quick but meaningful nod of approval for every success.

It was hard, dirty, and never-ending, but Trevor felt a sense of accomplishment he had never felt before. He could finally see how the drills, the discipline, and the reason for it all were all connected. They weren't just doing exercises; they were learning what it meant to be a soldier.

The platoon was tired, dirty, and sunburned by the end of the week, but something had changed. Red Phase was hard and even punishing, but it was also building relationships and skills that could only come from working collectively to solve problems. Trevor wiped the sweat and dirt from his eyes and felt the pain in every muscle. He couldn't help but smile even though he was tired.

He thought they were getting stronger, one drill, one skill, and one field exercise at a time.

By the middle of Red Phase, Trevor had started to see the same few people everywhere. They were his lifeline in a world of yelling drill sergeants and never-ending drills. He had quietly made friends with three other trainees over the past two weeks. They were all new, like him, but they somehow handled the stress with humor and toughness.

Harris was the first person he got close to. He was tall and skinny, and always had a crooked grin on his face. He was good at keeping things light even when the drill sergeants' voices sounded like thunder. Trevor admired how he could make everyone laugh with a joke or a quick comment. He had grown up in a small town in Georgia, where he played football and worked on his dad's farm. But there was a sharp mind behind the jokes. Harris learned quickly, picked up on small hints, and quietly pushed himself to stay at the front of the pack during drills.

At first glance, Lopez looked scary because he was stocky, strong, and disciplined. He moved with purpose, never wasted a step, and seemed to know right away how important each command was. Trevor had learned that Lopez was competitive and always pushed himself and the platoon to do their best. Lopez had a dry sense of humor and a protective streak. If someone fell during an obstacle, he was the first to steady them and give them a pep talk, even when the drill sergeants were watching.

Daniels was quieter than the others because he was a thinker. He was thin and wiry, and his dark eyes seemed to always be looking around and thinking about what they saw. He didn't talk much, but when he did, it was usually to point out a faster way to get across a muddy course or to remind someone of an important step in the hand-to-hand drills. Trevor admired Daniels for staying calm in the middle of the chaos. They had shared moments of laughter and frustration over time, and they had a deeper understanding of each other than words could say.

Trevor, Harris, Lopez, and Daniels all had a bond even though none of them talked about it. During the confidence obstacle course, they cheered each other on, helped each other when gear got stuck, and nodded quickly when the Drill sergeants yelled orders. They were all new, all inexperienced, and all trying to figure out how to stay alive, but somehow, in the middle of the heat, dirt, and constant drills, they had found something like friendship.

But not everyone got along with Trevor. There was Private Carter, a skinny kid from Ohio who was quick to speak and even quicker to get angry. Carter didn't like how Trevor made fun of his accent, questioned his strength, and tried to outdo him at every turn. While Trevor's friends told him to keep going, Carter tried to get to him.

Trevor tried to ignore him at first, but it was hard. Carter seemed to love competition, and it was clear that he wanted to show that he was better. The competition made everything more stressful, from marches and obstacle courses to the firing range. Trevor knew one thing: if Carter wanted to make him his enemy, Trevor would have to beat him the only way that mattered: by never giving up.

Trevor learned that people were important, even in boot camp where everyone was the same. These three friends were the anchors that kept him on track and moving forward. They reminded him he wasn't completely alone in this horrible world.

He thought, "We'll face whatever comes, side by side," as he looked at them across the muddy training field, one drill, one step, and one tiring day at a time.

Trevor's first mail day was already making his heart race. He was hoping to receive a letter from Alyssa. Finally, the Drill sergeant called his name. It sounded like thunder reverberating through the barracks.

Trevor's hands were sweaty, and he snapped to attention and marched toward the drill sergeant. The man held a small pile of letters and postcards and looked at the next name on his list. When Trevor took the mail, his stomach tightened. He walked back, careful not to drop anything.

There was a crisp envelope with handwriting he recognized and a return address he knew by heart. Alyssa.

He carefully ripped it open, almost as if he were worshiping it, and began to read. He felt warm and longing when she spoke. She wrote about how proud she was of him for getting this far, how much she missed him, and how often she thought about him. She told Trevor about little things that happened at home, funny things that happened at school, and the latest gossip from friends that made him laugh quietly to himself.

Alyssa's letter reminded him why he was there: she told him to keep going, stay strong, and never give up, even when things got too hard. She ended with a short but powerful message: "I love you, Trevor. Come back safe, and remember that we're all cheering for you."

Trevor's heart raced as he carefully folded the letter and put it in the front of his uniform. He could feel a grin spreading across his face, but as soon as he looked up, his friends saw it.

Harris leaned over and lightly elbowed him. "Well, well, well... it looks like someone is feeling a little more energetic!"

Lopez shook his head and smiled. "What is that? Your first letter of love? Didn't know you had it in you, Private."

Daniels, who was always quiet, just raised an eyebrow and smiled. "Be careful, man. Don't cry into your food tonight."

Trevor laughed, a little embarrassed, but he couldn't hide how excited he was. "Yeah, yeah, laugh it off. Alyssa sent it. She wrote about everything: school, home, and how much she misses me."

The teasing went on, but it was all in good fun. The letter reminded Trevor that people cared about him, waited for him, and believed in him outside of the harsh, unforgiving world of boot camp. That thought alone made the yelling, sweat, and dirt a little easier to deal with.

He thought, "One day at a time... letters like this make it

all worthwhile."

Trevor took out a blank piece of paper and started writing back after the lights went out and the barracks got quiet. He told Alyssa all about his first few weeks of training, including the obstacle courses, the confidence drills, getting used to the M16A2, and even the first field exercise, The Hammer. He talked about the sweat, the mud, the early mornings, and the times when he wanted to give up, but he kept going, step by step.

He talked about the little wins and the things he learned, making sure to say how her letter had made him feel better. Every word made him remember why he was there, why he had to go through the pain, and why he had to get stronger. He wrote about how much he missed her and how every memory of her made the hardest days a little easier to get through.

Trevor talked about his friends Harris, Lopez, and Daniels. He said they made him laugh when things got tough and that they all helped each other through the hardest drills. He wanted Alyssa to know he wasn't alone, even though he was far from home.

Finally, he signed the letter with all the emotion he could find: "Stay safe, write me back, and I'll come home stronger for you. I love you more than I can say."

He folded the letter neatly, put it in the envelope, and sealed it. He felt both relieved and sad. Even in boot camp, when it was hot, dirty, and drill sergeants were yelling at him, writing to her made him think of home, love, and everything he was fighting for.

He lay back on his bunk and stared at the ceiling for a moment, letting the quiet wash over him. "One day at a time," he whispered. "I'm doing this for us, Alyssa. Every drill, every obstacle I overcome, is for us."

# CHAPTER NINE

September 2000, Fort Knox

*W*eek Four was the start of White Phase, the last stage of Basic Combat Training. The initial shock of boot camp had started to wear off and the soldiers were settling into a routine, focusing on their work and feeling more like a team. Trevor saw small changes in the drill sergeants. They were still strict and bossy, but at times they showed appreciation and even respect when the platoon did well. Before, they hadn't recognized the hard work being done.

Physical training never stopped. There were road marches, runs, and strength exercises in the morning that made their muscles scream. But Trevor and his three friends Harris, Lopez, and Daniels were stronger now, both in body and mind. They cheered each other on as they climbed ropes, scaled high walls, and crossed parallel bars on the confidence course. They celebrated small wins that felt huge after weeks of being tired.

The basics of weapons became second nature. Trevor spent hours taking apart his M16A2 rifle, cleaning it, then putting it back together. He learned every click, every part, and every safety measure. The gun didn't scare him anymore and he carried it with confidence. It felt like a part of him.

By Week Five, shooting was the most important thing they did all day. They learned the basics of aiming, breathing, and staying focused by spending hours on the rifle range. Trevor did well because all his practice paid off in terms of accuracy. Squad movements and formations added tactical layers that got them ready for more difficult field exercises. Drills and ceremonies occurred often, and every march, salute, and movement was carefully watched for perfect execution.

During this week, Trevor saw Staff Sergeant Reynolds for the first time. Reynolds was different from some Drill sergeants who yelled all the time. He had a commanding presence and was fair, which earned him respect. Trevor liked how Reynolds pushed him and the rest of the platoon without being mean. He found himself paying more attention, learning faster, and even feeling a sense of respect that he hadn't expected.

The platoon had become a team by Week Six. Field training exercises pushed them to their limits with tactical maneuvers, camouflage, and fake combat movements, often with little sleep. Trevor had a lot more faith in his abilities now, and he depended on Harris, Lopez, and Daniels more than ever. They were no longer just friends; they were teammates who looked out for each other, pushed each other to do their best, and celebrated wins.

At the end of Week Six, combat testing showed how far they had come. The Drill sergeants looked at how well the soldiers could shoot, work as a team, and handle stress. As Trevor moved through the tests, he felt proud. His M16A2 was steady in his hands, his friends were close by, and the lessons he had learned in the past few weeks were paying off in real ways. Even the Drill sergeants nodded and gave a quick, approving look.

Trevor thought about how far they had come. The challenge had started out as scary and chaotic. Both sides had earned respect: the Drill sergeants had earned it from the platoon, and Trevor had earned it from Staff Sergeant Reynolds, whose fair and helpful leadership had made a lasting impression.

One drill, one lesson, one field exercise at a time, Trevor thought. We're getting closer and are ready for whatever comes next. The platoon got a rare reward that Sunday: a phone call home that lasted ninety minutes. The trainees had been free for the longest time since they got there, and as soon as the Drill sergeants said so, they lined up for the pay phones like they were gold. They waited their turn with calling cards in hand, eager to hear familiar voices.

When Trevor finally got into the booth and entered the numbers, his heart raced faster than it had on the rifle range. The call went through, and in a few seconds, he could hear his mother. He felt better.

Trevor talked to his mom and dad for the next twenty minutes about the crazy weeks he had just had at PT, the obstacle courses, the marksmanship training, and the long days in the field. Trevor's dad asked if he was doing okay, and Trevor told him that he was stronger than he had ever been. His mom, who was sad but proud, told him to stay safe, keep his head down, and believe in what he was learning. It felt like a warm blanket on a cold night.

As soon as it was time to switch, Trevor called Alyssa. His voice got softer as soon as she answered.

"Hey, it's me. I don't have much time, but it's so good to hear your voice."

Trevor told her everything for the rest of the call: how much he missed her, how he thought about her all the time, and how her letter had helped him through the hardest times. He asked her how school was going, if she was okay, and paid close attention to everything she said. He almost forgot where he was when he heard her laugh through the crackle of the pay phone.

He whispered, "I love you," near the end, holding on to the moment.

Alyssa said, "I love you too," in a steady voice full of longing. "Trevor, you're doing great things. Don't forget that."

The Drill sergeant finally said it was time to go, and Trevor hung up. He stepped away from the booth feeling homesick and determined at the same time. That ninety-minute call brought back memories of the family, love, and a future worth fighting for, and all of them waited for him outside Fort Knox.

By the seventh week, Trevor and the other members of his platoon were no longer the confused, scared recruits who got off the bus at Fort Knox. The Army had started to turn them into soldiers. PT still started before the sun came up in the mornings, but now it was almost second nature. Road marches lasted longer, rucksacks got heavier, and the tactical exercises required accuracy and working as one. But Trevor saw a difference now: what once seemed impossible, now seemed possible.

The Drill sergeants had changed too. They weren't easy on them, but the yelling had stopped. While mistakes were still punished with harsh discipline, there was a new sense of respect offered. He felt it the most from Staff Sergeant Reynolds, who was his favorite. Reynolds didn't give out praise easily, but when Trevor did a drill well or shot well on the range, the small nod of approval he received was enough to keep him going for days.

They went deeper into advanced infantry training in Week Eight. The long field exercises made it hard to remember the days spent digging fighting positions, moving through the woods in squad formations, learning to trust camouflage, and pushing through fatigue. It was hard and dirty work, but Trevor was proud of how far he had come. He could carry the ruck, move with his squad in a smart way, and keep his weapon ready without thinking twice. There wasn't much sleep at night in the field, but there were quiet times with Harris, Lopez, and Daniels, talking under the stars about home.

By Week Nine, everyone in the company was talking about one thing: Going green. The ceremony was the end of the Basic training part of OSUT, and it was the first time families could see how far their soldiers had come. Trevor thought about it to get through the hardest drills. For the first time in weeks, he let himself picture his mom and dad sitting in the stands with Alyssa, waiting for him.

The day finally came, and Trevor stood tall in formation

for the company's Turning Green ceremony. The green cords on their shoulders showed that they were no longer just trainees; they were now soldiers in the US Army.

Trevor saw them in the crowd: his mom and dad, waving proudly, and Alyssa next to them, her smile bright even from a distance. He tried to stay calm, but his heart was racing inside.

They were let go after the ceremony and the briefings. Trevor didn't even have time to catch his breath before his family wrapped him in their arms. His mom held him close and cried as she told him how proud she was of him. His dad shook his hand hard and then hugged him. And then Alyssa came along.

Trevor held her in his arms for the first time in months. He kissed her, hugged her tightly, and forgot about all the long days he had spent at Fort Knox. His voice broke as he whispered, "I missed you so much."

The weekend pass that came next was a present. They talked about family news, stories from training, and school updates from Alyssa. They laughed and cried, and Trevor wouldn't let go of her hand. He held Alyssa close whenever he could, remembering how her laugh sounded, how her hand felt in his, and how good it felt to be near her again.

It was sad to know that the time was short, but Trevor loved every second of it. The long days of OSUT had pushed him in ways he never thought possible, but now that he was with his family and Alyssa, he felt stronger than ever. He was no longer the scared teen who had left home; he was a soldier ready for what was to come.

Trevor wished he could bottle up the hugs, laughter, and quiet times that made up the weekend and take them with him. But it was over just as quickly as it started. The truth hit hard when it was time to go back to base. Families loaded up their cars, and soldiers gathered where the Drill sergeants told them to. Each soldier held on to their last moments of freedom.

Trevor hugged his mom and dad tightly. He could feel his mom's tears on his shoulder and his dad's strong hand squeezing the back of his neck. Alyssa came next. He kissed her one last time and held on longer than he should have, not wanting to let go.

"I'll write you," she said softly, her eyes shining.

"Yes, I know," Trevor said softly. "I'll be waiting for each letter."

Trevor stood tall as she drove away, forcing himself to stay in place while his family got into the car. He kept watching the taillights fade down the road until they were completely gone.

He knew he had come too far to quit now, even with the pain in his chest. The next phase of training would soon begin. In Advanced Individual Training (AIT), they would learn the specialized skills needed for their job. A new part. A new problem.

# CHAPTER TEN

November 2000, Fort Knox

*A*ll of weeks 10 through 17 were spent training for Cavalry Scout. Every head was given the same uniform buzz cut. The barracks became a home, loud and restless, with tightly stacked bunks and drill sergeants making sure discipline never slipped. Trevor's enemy in Basic, Private Jackson, was still there, always glaring and competing.

The training schedule never stopped. Morning PT was still hard, but the focus had changed. They were no longer just soldiers; they were becoming Scouts. Every day, they added new skills on top of the ones they already had. Trevor and the others learned how to do reconnaissance and security by moving quietly through the woods, studying the terrain, setting up observation posts, and reporting back without being seen.

The cavalry didn't just walk around on patrols. They learned about the M1 Abrams tank, the Bradley Fighting Vehicle, and the Humvee. The first time Trevor got into a Bradley, his heart raced. The steel walls hummed with power, and it felt like stepping into a beast ready to charge. Even the Humvees, which looked easy at first, were hard to drive off-road with their instructors watching.

Their weapons training now included the M4 rifle, the M9 pistol, the M240B machine gun, the M249 SAW, and even the huge.50 caliber machine gun, in addition to the M16A2. Trevor would always remember the first time he shot the gun. The 50 caliber recoil shook his shoulders, the roar echoed through his chest, and the weapon's power left him speechless, as if he were holding the fist of God.

The drill sergeants still yelled, but now things were different. They weren't just tearing down the trainees anymore; they were starting to build them up. Fear started to turn into respect. Trevor really liked Drill sergeant Ramirez. He was a tough but fair man who seemed more interested in making them into real Cavalry Scouts than punishing them for every mistake.

It was the letters, though, that helped Trevor get through those weeks. He looked forward to mail call every day. As if he were calling roll, the Drill sergeant would stand at the front of the formation and yell out names. Every soldier hoped for the best. Trevor's heart raced every time someone said his name, especially when it was Alyssa.

Her letters were the only thing keeping him alive. She wrote about school and her classes, how quiet everything was without him, and how much she missed him all the time. She talked about little things that happened during her days, like sitting with her friends at lunch, watching football games on Friday nights, and walking across campus with his hoodie over her shoulders when it got cold at night. Her handwriting sometimes looked rushed, like she had written down her thoughts quickly between classes to make sure they got sent on time. And every now and then, when he opened one of her envelopes he could smell something else on the paper that was faint, but unmistakable. Her perfume. It was as if she had held the paper close before sealing it. It sounded crazy, but when he put the pages up to his face in the dark of the barracks, it felt like she was right there with him, close enough to touch. He never told anyone that. It was his secret.

He wrote back whenever he could, usually late at night when the barracks lights were dim. His letters told her about his training, the weapons and vehicles, and how hard it all was. But they always ended the same way: he missed her, loved her, and was counting down the weeks until they could be together again.

If the platoon behaved well, they could use the phone every Sunday. There was a long line for the pay phones, and each soldier had a calling card in their hand. Trevor usually spent about ten minutes talking to his parents to let them know he was safe and tell them how things were going. Alyssa got the rest of the time, though. More than anything else, hearing her voice calmed him down. He'd tell her about his week at the Bradley, the long marches, and even the MREs they had to eat. She'd laugh and say she was proud, but she missed him a lot. They cried some Sundays and laughed other times, but they always ended with the same words: "I love you. Write back soon."

The weeks ran together in sweat, mud, and tiredness. Field training got longer and harder. Trevor and his platoon spent the night in the woods learning how to work in sync, set up security perimeters, and practice reconnaissance patrols. They often ate cold MREs on the go and slept in short, stolen bursts that were always cut short by the need for someone to keep watch.

The last test was a week-long field training exercise. They marched out with heavy backpacks, set up patrol bases, did reconnaissance missions, and fought fake enemies in fake combat operations. The days ran together in a fog of hunger, tiredness, and willpower. Trevor's body screamed at him to stop, but he kept going because he wanted to and because he knew graduation was just around the corner.

By the end of Week 17, Trevor looked back and saw how much he had changed since he got off the plane in Louisville as a scared kid. He was no longer just a trainee. He was a scout for the cavalry, and it was almost time to graduate after the months of training. Long days, late nights, and no breaks. He'd never forget this day, standing on the parade field in his dress uniform with his brothers-in-arms. Families cheered and cameras flashed as the new Cavalry Scouts marched across the field. The pride in the air was thick.

Alyssa was in the crowd. She had come, and when Trevor saw her, he felt both proud and relieved. He held her tightly after the ceremony, and neither of them wanted to let go. They both knew their time would be short.

They only had one day with their families, which was a short but important reunion. Trevor took in every second he spent with Alyssa and his family, knowing that he would be leaving the next morning. Hugs lasted a little longer, conversations went on until the last minute, and every look took on more meaning.

There was no time to waste the next morning. The new soldiers were already getting on buses and planes on their way to their first duty stations. Trevor's destination was Fort Carson, Colorado, where he would join the famous 3rd Armored Cavalry Regiment. From then on, he would wear the name "Brave Rifles" with pride as he became a Cavalryman, carrying Alyssa's love and the regiment's legacy with him.

The next morning came too soon. Trevor gave Alyssa one last hug before getting on another bus to the airport. He kept his head up even though his heart was heavy. When he got to the terminal, he was surprised that people he didn't know came up to him, shook his hand, and thanked him for his service. It was strange, humbling, and a little too much.

He got on his plane and it landed in Colorado Springs a few hours later. A shuttle took him straight to Fort Carson, home of the 3rd Armored Cavalry Regiment, also known as the Brave Rifles.

Processing was quick, but it was hard work. The afternoon was full of paperwork, gear checks, and short orientations. Finally, Trevor was taken to his assigned barracks. The building was old and smelled like floor wax and sweat. There were rows of bunk beds in his room, shared lockers, and bathrooms down the hall. At least there was a dining room close by where the soldiers could get a hot meal without having to walk all the way across base.

Trevor met his new roommates that first night. Morales was a big, loud Texan who seemed to know everyone and was quick to invite new people to play cards. Whitaker, on the other hand, was quiet and often kept to himself, reading or writing letters home. Kowalski was tall and thin, with a sarcastic side and a drive that made him go to the gym whenever he could. Delgado was always ready with a story about a girl from back home. He had a nice smile and a smooth way of talking. Then there was Henderson, a blunt, stubborn Georgian who acted like he had something to prove. Trevor and Henderson rarely agreed, and their words carried an edge, but the forced politeness between them kept the air from breaking outright—like a thread stretched tight, holding the tension at bay.

Even though they were all different, Trevor felt the unspoken bond that connected them. He unpacked his bag and slid it under the bunk. In that moment it hit him. *I'm going to be a Brave Rifle.*

Trevor's first week at Fort Carson went by so quickly he couldn't keep track of it. The moment he got there, the in-processing started. He went to the personnel section, S1, where there was a lot of paperwork waiting for him. Before he could really settle in, everything had to be in order: assignments, pay forms, medical updates, and so on. After that he got his orders, which were stamped and signed, linking his name to the 3rd Armored Cavalry Regiment.

He and the other new arrivals started to figure out where they would live when they got back to the barracks. The bunks were too small, the lockers were too small, and the bathrooms were always full, but Trevor quickly learned that this was just how things were in the Army. He learned the layout of the building and got used to the sound of boots shuffling through the hallways, as well as the rhythm of chow times and formations.

He felt like he was in a storm when he trained. The Brave Rifles were proud of their standards, and it showed. Trevor and his unit were out in formation every morning, pounding the pavement before the sun even rose over the Colorado Rockies. The runs got longer, the push-ups and sit-ups never stopped, and the cadre pushed them harder every day. It was clear what the message was: endurance was survival, and stamina was just as important as any weapon.

They met in the evenings for classes where they learned about the regiment's history and customs. Trevor paid close attention as the teachers talked about the Brave Rifles' long and interesting history, the battles they fought all over the world, and their proud motto: "Blood and Steel." The words moved him. He was no longer just a soldier; he was part of a legacy.

There was a problem with the equipment in the middle of the week. As the supply sergeants handed out uniforms, gear, and other specialized tools, Trevor stood in line with the others. His rucksack slowly filled with the tools he needed for his job. After that, he met the men and women who would be in charge of his squadron and troop, the people who would shape his future in the regiment. The introductions were short but important, and each handshake was a step closer to his new life.

Training got better by the end of the week. Trevor got to see the M1 Abrams tanks and Bradley Fighting Vehicles that made up the regiment for the first time. At first, their size and power were too much to handle, but there was no denying the rush of pride that came from getting in one. Along with getting to know the vehicle, they learned tactics for scout reconnaissance, security operations, and maneuvers to find and fix an enemy. It was hard work that required a lot of thought, and Trevor knew he was only getting started.

He started to look around Fort Carson itself when he wasn't on duty. The base was huge and had its own PX, commissary, gyms, and places to relax. It was like a small city, and Trevor had to learn how to get around, where to eat, where to relax, and where to get what he needed. He began to feel more like he belonged and less like an outsider.

But when the noise of the day died down and the barracks got quiet, Trevor felt something else. He was starting to miss Alyssa more than he expected. He couldn't stop thinking about her smile, her laugh, and even the way her letters smelled like her perfume. He lay on the bunk at night, surrounded by strangers who were quickly becoming brothers. He wished she was here with him.

Trevor was tired by the end of the first week. His body hurt from all the work and his head was full of new information. But there was pride under the tiredness and the desire for Alyssa. He was no longer just Trevor from home; he was a Brave Rifle, following in the footsteps of many others who had carried the name before him. And this was just the start.

# CHAPTER ELEVEN

December 2000, Fort Carson

*T*hat first week in the Brave Rifles was hard, but by Friday Trevor felt a little better. That morning, he went to the PX and bought a simple, sturdy Nokia phone that felt like it weighed a lot in his hand. He had been waiting for this call since he graduated.

He said, "Alyssa?" and tried to keep his voice steady. "I'm not working this weekend... I want you to come out. We can stay at a hotel nearby, and I'll pay for the flight and everything."

There was a pause on the line and then her voice, warm and bright, made him smile even though he was stressed out from the week. "I'll be there," she said without any other words.

Finally, the weekend came, and with it came the excitement Trevor had been looking forward to all week. As soon as Alyssa got off the shuttle after flying in, it felt like the distance between them was gone. After a quick hug and coffee that felt like it lasted forever, they set off to see the beauty of Colorado.

Their first stop was the Garden of the Gods, where huge

red rock formations stood out against the clear blue sky. They laughed as they walked along the winding paths, trying to balance on the rocks and daring each other to take silly pictures. After that, they drove up to Pikes Peak. The wind blew around them as they took in the stunning views from the top. Trevor couldn't stop smiling as Alyssa leaned in close to share in the beauty of the land.

The next day, they walked around the Cheyenne Mountain Zoo, amazed by the animals as they joked about who would last longer if they were thrown into the wild. Later, they went into the Cave of the Winds, where they explored the cool, dark caves and felt a thrill at the hidden beauty below. They talked about everything at each stop, their hopes, fears, and the future they wanted to share. The space was filled with laughter and quiet moments of closeness.

Trevor and Alyssa didn't waste a single moment that first night in the hotel room. They held each other close, whispered, and laughed, letting their feelings take over. They rolled around on the sheets, wrapped in each other's arms, their hearts racing and their breaths mixing. They were completely lost in the warmth and closeness they had been craving. For those hours, time seemed to stand still. The outside world didn't exist; it was just them, their love, and the bond that had carried them across every mile apart.

Trevor and Alyssa sat on the couch next to each other, the soft glow of the city lights coming in through the window. They had just had a quiet moment at the hotel. He took a deep breath and felt the weight of what he was about to say.

He started, "I've been thinking..." with a little hesitation in his voice. "What if you got closer? You could go to the

University of Colorado in Colorado Springs and live on campus. We wouldn't just be together on weekends.

Alyssa turned to him and looked for his eyes. "Move here?" she asked softly, as if she were trying out the idea in her head.

Trevor said, "Yes," and reached for her hand. "I want us to be able to see each other more often, without all the space between us. I know it's a big deal, but... I believe it could work. Alyssa, I want you close. I miss you too much when you're not here."

She smiled, and her face showed a mix of excitement and nervousness. She said, "I've thought about it too. And... I think I could do it. I could move here, go to UCCS, and live on campus. Even if it's not on base, we'd still see each other a lot."

Trevor's chest rose as she spoke. "Really?" he asked, unable to believe what he heard.

"Really," she said as she squeezed his hand. "We'll figure it out. I want to be with you."

Trevor felt closer to her than he had since leaving home, not just in miles, but also in the promise of their future. The weekend had brought them closer, and now that Alyssa was making plans to move closer, it felt like they were starting a new chapter.

Sunday morning came too soon. The truck was quiet except for the soft hum of the engine as Trevor drove Alyssa to the airport. They hugged tightly at the gate and kissed for a short time, neither wanting to let go. After she boarded,

Trevor stayed, watching her plane taxi and take off from the window.

He watched until it was just a dot against the clouds. As he turned away, a quiet thought came to him. "I hope she decides to attend UCCS. I guess time will tell."

A few weeks went by with days full of the never-ending training, paperwork, and learning how to be a Brave Rifle. Trevor still found time to call Alyssa every night, and their voices crossed the miles between them. One night, while he was wiping the sweat off his face after a long day of PT, the phone rang. Alyssa. Her voice made his world light up.

With a hint of excitement she said, "I've been talking to the university about the process of transferring to UCCS, and it looks good!"

Trevor smiled, his heart racing with excitement. "That's incredible!" he said. "I can't wait for you to get closer. This is... it's amazing."

She laughed softly, but there was still a hint of doubt in her voice. "My parents don't like the idea, but they get it. They know we want it, and they're doing their best to help."

Trevor felt a rush of joy. He felt energized and hopeful at the thought of having Alyssa close by and seeing her more than just on weekends and holidays. He smiled to himself and said, "I'm so excited. I can't wait for this to happen."

Even though there were problems ahead, that talk made

him feel better, more focused, and excited about the future they were slowly building.

Another week came and went, and life as a Brave Rifle began to feel normal. Days were long but well-organized, with a steady mix of hands-on training and classroom lessons. Every morning, the Bradley Fighting Vehicles would get Preventive maintenance checks and Services. The soldiers crawled under the big machines and checked every bolt and system to make sure each vehicle was ready for whatever the regiment might face. Sometimes it was boring work, but Trevor knew it was necessary for the safety of the crew and the mission.

They spent their afternoons at the firing range practicing drills with their gear and learning how to use weapons. Trevor's confidence grew as he did each exercise, which tested his endurance, focus, and ability to work as a team. There were also lectures and classes on tactics, how to drive vehicles, and the finer points of armored reconnaissance.

The pace changed for the better in the evenings. He spent his free time with his battle buddies, who were quickly becoming like family to him. They went to the bowling alley where they cheered each other on and made fun of each other's gutter balls and strikes. The barracks lounge was filled with laughter as cards were dealt. The stakes were low, but the friendship was strong. They would sometimes just hang out, tell stories, talk about home, and make jokes until the lights went out and it was time for bed.

Trevor felt the same mix of tiredness and happiness by the end of the week. The work was hard, and the training never stopped, but he could see himself getting stronger, smarter, and better at what he did every day. In the evenings, when he was with friends and laughing, he felt like he belonged, which made it all worth it.

On Saturday morning, Trevor's phone rang, and a voice he knew made his day. "Trevor! I made it in!" Alyssa yelled, and her excitement was so strong that it almost crackled through the line.

"What? Really?" he said, almost dropping the phone.

"Yes!" she said with a laugh. "I'm going to UCCS! It feels like the pieces are finally falling into place.

Trevor's smile went from one ear to the other. He was so excited he could hardly hold it in. "Wow, Alyssa, that's great! I can't wait for you to get here!"

She smiled, but he couldn't see it because they were on the phone. She said, "I'll be there near the end of the month. I'll have to take some summer classes to get back on track, but it'll be worth it. We will finally be close to each other."

Trevor was happy and relieved all at once. The idea of having her around all the time, not just on weekends, made the long days and hard work at Fort Carson seem easier. "I'm so excited," he said. "I can't wait for you to come."

Trevor couldn't stop smiling even after the call was over. He was beginning to feel like things were real, and the thought of seeing Alyssa soon made each day a little better.

The month went by quickly, with the days blending into the routine of training, maintenance, and the quiet excitement of Alyssa's arrival. It was finally time for her to move into her dorm at UCCS over the weekend. This was the start of her journey toward a bachelor's degree in teaching.

Her parents drove up to the campus with boxes, suitcases, and all the little things that made a dorm feel like home. Trevor met them in the parking lot, feeling both excited and nervous. There was always some tension when he met her parents, but the visit went surprisingly well. They were polite and even friendly, but they quietly watched Trevor as he helped her carry her things inside.

Kowalski, one of Trevor's friends from his platoon, had also offered to help. He made the heavy lifting and unpacking almost fun with his usual sarcastic humor and laid-back attitude. They all worked to get Alyssa comfortable in her room by moving furniture around, stacking boxes, and making jokes.

Trevor stepped back and looked around the dorm once it was clean. He saw Alyssa smile at the room she would now call home. It was a small but important moment that showed their lives were starting to come together. There was a lot going on at the start of the weekend, but by the end of the day, Trevor was very happy and excited for the next few months, knowing that Alyssa would be only a short drive away.

The sun was starting to go down behind the campus buildings by the time Alyssa's dorm was all set up. She unpacked boxes, put the shelves in order, and for the first time, the space really felt like hers. Trevor stepped back and watched her smile as she ran her hand over her neatly made bed. He felt proud and happy.

They leaned against the window and looked out over the campus for a few quiet minutes. Alyssa said softly, "It feels so real now." Her eyes sparkled.

Trevor nodded and held her hand tightly. When he spoke, his voice was full of relief and excitement. "Yes, it does. And now we're really going to be close."

He said goodbye later that night and drove back to Fort Carson and his job as a Brave Rifle with a smile he couldn't hide. He took with him the warmth of the weekend, the promise of seeing her often, and the thought that their lives were finally starting to take shape. He drove back to the base with a smile he couldn't hide. For the first time since leaving home, the distance didn't seem too far, and the future seemed full of possibilities with Alyssa nearby.

# CHAPTER TWELVE

February 2001, Fort Carson

*A*s the weeks went by, Trevor's and Alyssa's friends started hanging out with them. Maya, Jenna, and Sophie, Alyssa's close friends at UCCS, and Travor's battle buddies slowly joined them for outings.

They'd all spend weekends hanging out in Colorado Springs to try out the city's cool local restaurants, hike at Garden of the Gods or Pikes Peak, and go to the movies. They became a close-knit group and did everything from college parties where the music and laughter was loud, to quiet parks where they could sit and talk. They bowled, played cards, told jokes, took late-night drives under the stars, and celebrated the little wins in life with a sense of freedom Trevor hadn't felt in years.

The feeling of friendship went beyond just having fun and playing games. Every weekend trip, every hike, and every meal with friends reminded Trevor how much better his life had gotten. The Army had given him discipline and a sense of purpose, but it had also given him important people, experiences that pushed him, and a love that kept him grounded.

Kowalski immediately liked Maya. Their bond was instant,

full of teasing, laughter, and the adventures they had. They quickly became an official couple, which led to a lot of double dates. The two couples often hiked at Garden of the Gods or Pikes Peak, ate at some of the city's coolest local restaurants, and even went to the movies once in a while.

The group dynamic added a new level of fun to their weekends. Trevor and Kowalski's battle buddies shared stories, and Trevor enjoyed the moments even more when he saw Alyssa happy and relaxed with her friends. The harsh Colorado winter didn't stop them from having fun; the cold air made their get-togethers feel warmer, which was a nice change from the strict schedules at Fort Carson.

One week, Trevor noticed Kowalski acting strangely. During one of their breaks, they sat on a bench near the barracks and Kowalski began telling him about the tension he'd been feeling with Maya. How the small misunderstandings, jealousy, and miscommunication between them was getting on his nerves. Trevor helped Kowalski see things in a different way by giving him good advice and telling him the truth. Kowalski's shoulders felt lighter by the end of the conversation, and he was ready to talk to Maya again.

That Friday night was the perfect time for a double date. Trevor, Alyssa, Kowalski, and Maya went to a party at their college. Trevor had never seen anything like this before. The house was full of energy and excitement, with loud music playing and a keg sitting off to the side. It was a world away from the strict, orderly life at Fort Carson. It was busy, loud, and full of life.

They talked, laughed, and shared stories with other

students. They felt like they were both part of the crowd and separate from it, but they were connected by how comfortable they were with each other. Alyssa's hand in Trevor's felt like a lifeline in the chaos of college life. He smiled as he watched Kowalski and Maya joke and tease each other from across the room.

Later, as the night came to an end, they went back to Alyssa and Maya's dorm. The room in the apartment was quiet now, which was very different from the party. Trevor and Alyssa found a quiet moment, holding each other close and enjoying the closeness that had seemed fleeting during the week. They whispered to each other and touched each other gently while wrapped up in each other's arms, feeling the warmth of each other as if the world outside had disappeared.

It was hard for Trevor to believe. After weeks of being apart, following strict schedules, and being pulled away by training, he and Alyssa could finally be together. They could feel every heartbeat, every breath, and every small change in emotion. They were both tired but happy the next day, with memories of connection, love, and closeness that kept Trevor grounded as he returned to his duties.

There was a feeling of renewal and energy in the air as spring came to Colorado Springs. These past few months has been the best of Trevor's life. One afternoon, he stood outside the barracks, feeling the sun on his face and listening to the trees rustling in the breeze. He thought about how far he'd come. It was a hard decision to join the Army, but now he knew it was the right choice. No more worrying about old bills, no more jobs that lead nowhere, and no more not knowing what to do. He had a purpose, a plan, and a group of friends who were like family.

Alyssa was the most important thing in his life. The distance that once seemed impossible to cross was gone. Instead, they had stolen weekends, shared meals, and the quiet joy of being able to see each other almost whenever they wanted. They had a routine of small adventures and big moments, like exploring the Garden of the Gods trails, driving up to Pikes Peak, laughing at the mistakes they made on a casual hike, and taking in the stunning views that made every step worth it. Going to the movies or cafés made even the simplest outings feel special.

Trevor felt very thankful as he looked out at the blooming trees and the mountains in the distance. He had taken the leap and faced the challenge. In return, life had given him friends, adventure, and Alyssa, the most important thing of all.

For Trevor, spring was more than just a time of year. It was a party to celebrate change, growth, and it seems that everything feels like it's lining up the way it should be.

Trevor's phone rang loudly, and his heart raced even before he saw who it was. He answered, "Alyssa?" His voice was groggy, but when he heard her voice, it caught in his throat. She was scared, shaking, and crying so hard she couldn't stop.

"Trevor, it's my dad. He's... he's gone. He had a massive heart attack." Her words came out in a broken, jagged way between her sobs.

"Oh my God, Alyssa... I'm really sorry! What should I do?" Trevor asked, fighting to

steady his voice.

"Could you come over?" she whispered, her words catching in her throat. "I... I'm going home now."

"Yes," he said quickly, swallowing hard. "I'll buy your ticket. I'll pay for everything."

"Okay." There was a pause, followed by another sob. "Will you come with me?"
Trevor's throat tightened. He'd seen it happen to others, the Army never let anyone leave early. "I can't get out until Friday night," he said softly, "but I'll be there. I promise."

After she hung up, there was a shocked silence in the barracks room. Trevor sat on the edge of his bunk, staring at the phone in his hand. He felt both helpless and heartbroken. He couldn't be there for her when she needed him. He thought he was letting her down in the worst way possible.

Finally, it was Friday night. Trevor got on his flight with a lot of worry and regret on his mind. When his plane landed in St. Louis, his dad picked him up and drove him right to Alyssa's house. Before he even stepped inside, the air was thick with sadness. Seeing Alyssa and her family made him very sad. Her mother's quiet tears, her siblings' shocked faces, and the empty, aching space where her father should have been all made him feel sad.

But there was something wrong with Alyssa. She was distant and pulled away from Trevor. He couldn't get through to her. He was so desperate to know why he gently cornered her in the kitchen and took her hands in his. "Alyssa, is everything okay? Talk to me."

She had tears in her eyes, but her voice was sharp and shaky. "No! I needed you, Trevor, but you weren't here!"

Trevor's chest got tight. "I'm really sorry. I wanted to be here, but I couldn't leave the base. I really tried."

But she couldn't hear what he said. She shook her head and stepped back, then ran away from him with tears on her face. Trevor stood still for a moment, feeling empty, hopeless, and completely powerless. He tried to follow her, comfort her, and hold her, but nothing he did seemed to help. The funeral was sad and full of grief, and Trevor stayed as long as he could, silently supporting her from a distance and feeling every pang of her pain as if it were his own.

They drove to the airport after it was over. It was hard to breathe in the car with all the tension.

Alyssa's voice was soft but firm. "Trevor... I need some time off. I need some time to deal with this. I'll call you when I can."

Trevor nodded and swallowed, his throat tight. "Okay," he said quietly, barely able to talk.

Trevor walked into the terminal, forcing himself not to look back. By the time he sank into his seat on the plane, he could only stare blankly out the window as the engines thundered to life. There was one tear on his cheek. He was full of guilt, grief, and fear and couldn't help thinking, "I might lose her." The thought gnawed at him as the plane rose into the sky, taking him back to Fort Carson and leaving a piece of his heart with Alyssa.

During the next month the days were long and heavy. Alyssa stayed home, still distant and closed off, and Trevor felt helpless. He tried everything: calls, texts, letters, and even late-night talks, but nothing seemed to get through to her. He couldn't leave the base; but he wanted to be there for her when she needed him most. Every day that went by without a breakthrough made him feel like he was failing her.

Then, one night, the phone rang. Seeing her name on the screen made him feel both hopeful and scared. He answered right away.

"Trevor..." Alyssa's voice was low, but there was a determination in it that made his stomach turn. "I'm coming back." Please pick me up at the airport.

"Of course," he said quickly, trying to keep his voice steady. "Not a problem. See you in the morning. I love you." Before he could say anything else, she hung up. Trevor stared at the phone for a long time, feeling both disbelief and relief, but also a fear that wouldn't go away. That's great... I lost her, he thought, his heart racing.

He got to the airport early the next day and looked at every passenger who arrived. When he saw her, everything came into focus. When Alyssa's eyes met his, he ran to her without thinking and hugged her tightly. "I love you," he whispered. "I missed you so much."

She held onto him tightly, and her shoulders shook with silent tears. Trevor held her for as long as she needed, feeling her pain and stress flow into his chest. He wanted to take it all away, but he knew that some of it she had to deal with on her own.

As they drove to campus in the truck, she didn't say anything at first. She just stared out the window, and tears streamed down her face. He reached out to hold her hand, but she just leaned against the door and cried.

Trevor parked the truck in the dorm parking lot, and they sat there for a while, just breathing and letting the quiet of the evening wash over them. At last, Alyssa spoke.

"I'm sorry," she said, her voice breaking. "I was far away... I just didn't know what to do."

"I get it, Alyssa. I'm here for you no matter what." Every line on Trevor's face showed the honesty of his words. "Always."

She flinched, almost breaking. "Yeah, right," she said under her breath, still feeling hurt and doubtful.

"I know," he said quietly. "I wasn't there for you right away. But the Army... Without permission, I can't just leave. They said no. I'm sorry. I wanted to be there. I wanted to hold you right away when you needed me."

Her eyes softened, but the tears were still there. "I get it...

I really do," she said, her voice small but steady. "I love you."

He felt better and put his arm around her again. They stayed in the truck for a few more minutes to let the stress go down before finally getting out. Trevor went with her to her dorm room. Maya, Jenna, and Sophie, her friends, were there. They gave her a group hug and waved him away so they could have their reunion. He nodded, knowing that Alyssa needed some time alone. He let her go with her friends and turned to leave.

He felt a quiet sense of satisfaction and hope as he walked away. Things seemed like they might finally be okay for the first time in weeks.

Trevor stayed in the parking lot for a few minutes after Alyssa went into her dorm. He let out a deep breath he didn't know he had been holding. The worry, helplessness, and fear of losing her that had been weighing on him for the past month seemed to lift a little. He knew the road ahead wouldn't be easy and that grief and distance still hung over them like a shadow, but for the first time in weeks, he felt a spark of hope.

The air on campus was fresh and fragrant with blooming trees and new grass. Trevor looked up at the sky and felt like it reflected the new beginning between them. He had learned how to be patient and strong, and that love can grow stronger when things get tough.

That night was a turning point for him. He knew he couldn't change the past or take away the pain, but he could be there for Alyssa, strong and steady. He walked back to his truck, the city lights shining off the pavement, and whispered to himself, "We'll get through this, in unison."

CHAPTER THIRTEEN

September 2001, Fort Carson

S even months passed since the storm of grief and distance, and you could feel the subtle change in the air. Fall was starting to creep into Colorado Springs, tinting the trees with gold and amber and making the mornings crisp, which hinted at the changing season. Trevor and Alyssa's lives had settled into a routine based on their duties and the strong bond between them that had grown even stronger through hard times.

Alyssa was now a sophomore at UCCS. She was getting used to her classes, making new friends, and enjoying the freedom that comes with being in college. Trevor, on the other hand, kept living the disciplined life of a Cavalry Scout at Fort Carson, going through the tough routines, physical training, and maintenance work that made up his days. The Army took a lot of his time, focus, and energy, but it also gave him structure, a sense of purpose, and the strength to get through tough times at work and in his personal life.

The last seven months hadn't been easy. Alyssa's father's death left a quiet ache between them, a reminder of how fragile life is and how heavy its blows can be. But the experience also brought them closer. Every phone call, every weekend, every small moment they carved out only strengthened their bond. Their hiking trips, forays into local shops, and the easy rhythm of being with friends never seemed to get old. Even in the quiet stretches sitting on the floor of a dorm room or in the back of Trevor's truck, they could talk for hours about their hopes, fears, and the future ahead.

When fall came, Trevor felt happy and thankful. While he missed Alyssa when he was at Fort Carson, he was also happy in a quiet way. Life had changed, and things had tested them, but they were stronger, closer, and more sure than ever that they had built something worth keeping.

It was just another day at Fort Carson. Trevor was in the shop and crouched next to a Bradley Fighting Vehicle, checking the hydraulics and tightening bolts. The smell of grease and metal was all around him. The bay doors let in a lot of light in the morning, which made long shadows on the concrete floor. The sound of tools clanging and machines humming softly was the background noise of everyday life.

Then, out of nowhere, the bay doors flew open. One of the mechanics came running in, his face pale and his eyes wide, yelling over the noise. "Plane hit the World Trade Center! You have to see this!"

His words hung in the air like the aftermath of a shockwave. Trevor stood up straight, wiped his hands on a rag, and walked with the others to the small TV on the wall. The picture on the screen was surreal; smoke pouring from the tower, flames licking the sides of the building, and grainy news footage of the chaos. The group fell silent as they realized how big the situation was.

It was 09:03. They stood still and watched as the second plane hit, the horror happening in real time. The soldiers felt anger and disbelief. They quickly learned that the planes had been hijacked and this was not an accident, but a terrorist attack meant to shake the country to its core.

Trevor's phone rang, breaking the tense silence. He picked it up right away. "Alyssa?"

Her voice shook. "Do you see this?"

"Yes," Trevor said, his voice tight with disbelief. "I... I can't believe it."

They talked for a short time, sharing their shock and fear, but neither could fully understand how terrible the situation was. His fellow soldiers were quiet around him. Some stared at the screen, others whispered angrily to each other. In just an instant, nothing seemed normal anymore. The familiar clang of metal and engines and the regular maintenance tasks seemed small and far away compared to what just happened.

The soldiers in the shop weren't just going through another day of training. The air in the bay felt heavier, full of fear, determination, and the unspoken knowledge that what they were watching would change their lives, their mission, their country, and the world... forever.

For Cavalry Scouts at Fort Carson, the attacks on September 11, 2001, changed their daily lives in a big way right away. Within hours, security measures were put in place all over the base. Checkpoints were made stricter, ID checks were more thorough, and access to sensitive areas was tightly controlled. Soldiers who were used to the routines of training and maintenance suddenly became more alert because they knew that the world they had known was no longer safe. There were regular official briefings that went over the details of the attacks, named the people responsible, and talked about the Army's first response. The tone was serious and sad, but it was clear that the Army's mission had changed. What was once a peacetime schedule of training exercises and rotations changed to a faster pace. Planning for possible deployments, quick mobilization, and getting ready for combat operations became the new normal.

On a personal level for Trevor and the other Cavalry Scouts, their lives changed from routine drills, maintaining vehicles, and taking breaks on the weekends to getting ready for the Global War on Terrorism. It was a turning point that would shape their military careers and personal lives for years to come. They would always remember that things would never be the same.

That weekend, Trevor and Alyssa found time to be alone. They sat on a bench near the campus green with the cool fall air rustling the leaves around them. With the thought of what had happened, there was a new, unspoken worry in the air.

Trevor took her hand and felt how tense it was. "Alyssa... with everything that's happened, I might have to go to war soon," he said softly, choosing his words carefully. "I don't know when or for how long, but we need to think about it."

A flash of fear crossed Alyssa's face, and her eyes widened. "Deployed?" she whispered, her voice shaking. "Trevor, I

just lost my dad. I don't think I could handle losing you too."
She held his hands tighter, her knuckles turning white.

Trevor gently pulled her closer and put his arms around
her. "I know," he said, his own chest tight with worry. "I
don't want to leave you either. But I need to be ready. We
both need to be strong, even if it's hard. I promise I'll do
everything I can to get back to you."

Alyssa leaned her head against his shoulder and breathed
in and out shakily. "I'm just so scared, Trevor. What if
something goes wrong? What if you aren't here?"

Trevor kissed the top of her head and held her tighter. "I
can't control everything, Alyssa. But I can choose how much
I love you and how hard I will fight to come back. We'll face
whatever comes, side by side.

She nodded against him, tears streaming down her face.
She was scared, sad, and in love. "Okay," she said softly. "I
love you."

Trevor said, "I love you too," and then he pressed his
forehead to hers. At that moment, even though they were
scared and unsure of what was going to happen, they found a
fragile comfort in each other. It reminded them that their
bond was strong enough to survive distance and danger.

Two years went by in a flash. As a Cavalry Scout at Fort
Carson, Trevor's life continued with the same routines of
physical training, maintenance checks, and field exercises, and
on weekends and holidays he was with Alyssa. He stayed

sharp and got used to his job. Friends, fellow soldiers, and even his own leaders thought a deployment was coming, so it was a relief to Trevor when he never got an order to deploy.

In March 2003, though, everything changed. He got orders to Iraq for Operation Iraqi Freedom. He felt a rush of adrenaline and determination as he held the official papers in his hands. This is it, he thought. This is what I've been training for. All the years of hard work have finally come together for a reason.

But even in the excitement, he felt a knot in his chest. He thought of Alyssa right away. She was just starting her last year at UCCS, which was an important time for both her studies and her life. He was worried about leaving her behind, even though he knew she was strong and independent. He ran a hand over his face and thought, "She's going to be heartbroken." He was excited and proud to finally be deployed, but he also knew that the long months ahead would be hard on both of them.

Trevor's mind raced with ideas about how he would tell her, how they would deal with the distance, and how he could make her feel better about the fact that he would be back. For the first time in months, he felt the familiar mix of fear and excitement hit him hard. It reminded him that the life he had built at Fort Carson and the love he shared with Alyssa were about to be tested in ways they couldn't have imagined.

Trevor and Alyssa sat on the edge of her dorm bed that night, the soft light from a desk lamp casting shadows on the walls. The air between them was heavy with the news he had given her earlier. A folded paper with Trevor's deployment orders sat on the desk, a silent reminder of the truth that neither of them wanted to face.

"Alyssa..." Trevor said carefully as he took her hand in his. "I'll be gone by the end of the month. I won't be able to see you before we go. They just won't let me. We need to leave Fort Carson right away."

Alyssa's eyes got big and she swallowed hard. She tried to talk, but her lips shook and only a small, choked sound came out. She felt a rush of fear and anxiety in her chest. "You're just going to leave?" she asked, her voice shaking. "Not say goodbye? No... no time to just be together?"

Trevor shook his head, and his own heart began to hurt. "I wish it were different. I really do. I dreamed about this moment for so long, about finally doing the job I trained for, but there's nothing I can do. The orders are very strict. I can't get permission to leave early, and they won't change the rules."

Alyssa's hands gripped his tightly, as if holding on could keep him from leaving. "Trevor, I'm scared. I don't know what I'm going to do about this. You're leaving, and I just can't believe it." Her voice broke, and tears fell down her face.

Trevor pulled her close and held her against his chest. "I know, Alyssa. I know it's scary. I feel it too. But we'll make it through. We have to believe this distance won't tear us apart and that we'll stay in touch. I'll be thinking of you the whole time and I will write, call, or text you. You are always with me, no matter where I am."

She leaned against him and let out a shaky breath. "I'm

just... I'm scared. What if something goes wrong? What if you don't come back?"

Trevor held her face in his hands and looked straight into her eyes. "I'll be back. I can't promise it will be easy, but I can promise that I will do everything I can to come back to you. And when I do, we'll make up for all the time we've been apart. Alyssa, you've been my rock for the past few years. I need you to hold on to that, even when I'm not here."

She shook her head against him and he could hear her crying. She said softly, "I love you."

He put his forehead against hers and said, "I love you too. More than anything. And that won't change, not for a second."

They stayed like that for a long time, the dorm room was quiet except for the occasional sobs and steady breathing. They were both trying to hold on to each other before the storm of deployment tore them apart.

Trevor picked up the phone and called his parents. He gripped the receiver tightly as he waited for them to pick up. Trevor took a deep breath when he heard his dad's voice, which was steady and familiar.

"Mom and Dad, I got my orders to go to war. I leave at the end of March for Operation Iraqi Freedom." He paused to let the words sink in. "I know this will be hard for you too, but I need to ask you something. Please tell Alyssa if you hear any bad news about me while I'm gone. They won't officially tell her because we're not married, but I want her to know if anything happens. I trust you to keep her safe the way you've always kept me safe."

His parents were quiet for a moment, letting the weight of the request sink in, before they responded with quiet understanding. Trevor hung up, feeling the weight of both his duty and the distance that lay ahead.

On the morning of departure, Trevor stood in the barracks feeling both excited and scared. His gear, packed and polished, sat beside him and the familiar weight of his uniform grounded him in the reality of what was to come. His battle buddies moved around him with the same sense of purpose, joking to hide their own nerves, checking their vehicles, and getting ready for the flight to Iraq.

Trevor felt a rush of pride because he was trained, ready, and able to serve his country. This moment had come after every drill, every long day in the sun, every maintenance check, and every patrol exercise. And yet, even though he felt sure of himself, he was also scared of what he would face overseas and what he was leaving behind.

He thought of Alyssa's face, her smile, her laugh, and the quiet times they had in Colorado Springs. The idea of leaving her, even for a short time, made his chest feel like it was being squeezed. He had done everything he could to get ready for this, but nothing could prepare him for how much he missed her and how much he worried that she would miss him as much as he missed her.

He took a deep breath and ran his fingers over the insignia on his uniform. He silently promised himself and her that he would come back. The plane was waiting with its engines running, taking him and his friends into the unknown. Trevor took one last look at the barracks, which had become like a second home to him, and had one last thought of Alyssa. Then he squared his shoulders, held his head high, and stepped forward.

He was ready to serve and had trained for the mission, but no amount of preparation could make him forget the fear, longing, and love he felt. He didn't know what the future held, but he knew one thing for sure: no matter how far away they were, his heart would always belong to Alyssa.

# CHAPTER FOURTEEN

April 2003, Kuwait

*T*he Brave Rifles, or the 3rd Cavalry Regiment, had finished their last preparations in Kuwait by the middle of the month. Trevor and the other Cavalry Scouts checked their gear one last time, looked over maps, and went over mission briefings. The air was tense and full of anticipation. They knew the stakes were high. This deployment, Operation Iraqi Freedom I, was not just another rotation; it was a key part of the early campaign to bring down Saddam Hussein's government.

The regiment crossed the border into Iraq and rolled into Al Anbar Province with precision and determination. It was clear what they had to do: protect and stabilize the western part of the country, which was very important for the success of the first U.S. invasion. Trevor felt like he was in a dream. After years of training, he was finally here, part of a historic operation that would change the course of the war.

The landscape went on forever, with desert plains, small villages, and the hot sun overhead. Each Bradley Fighting Vehicle in the convoy moved with careful discipline, showing that the regiment was ready and professional. The soldiers were alert, focused, and ready for whatever problems might come their way.

Trevor's thoughts of Alyssa were always on the edge of his mind, a link to home that gave him strength even as the reality of war settled around him. The Brave Rifles had begun their mission, and with each mile they traveled into Al Anbar Province, they felt more and more responsible. This was no longer practice or training; it was real, and every choice and every action could mean the difference between life and death.

The first few days in Al Anbar Province were a harsh wake-up call about what war is really like. The desert went on forever, dry and harsh, with sand whipping across the roads and the sun beating down without mercy. Trevor quickly got used to the deployment routine, which included checking on the Bradley vehicles before dawn, going over intelligence reports, and patrolling towns and villages where the locals watched from a distance.

Every day was a mix of stress and routine. The soldiers did regular maintenance on their vehicles, practiced tactical maneuvers, and ran simulations to make sure every response was automatic. They had trained for this, but the environment was unpredictable, there were hidden threats, allegiances were uncertain, and there was always the chance of an ambush, which kept their senses sharp.

Trevor's mind kept going back to Alyssa through it all. During quiet times, he would sit in the Bradley and look out over the desert, imagining her at UCCS, walking around campus, meeting friends, laughing, and studying. He missed how warm she was, how she was always there for him, and how she had kept him grounded in the past few months.

Letters and calls were nice, but they could never replace the comfort of holding her hand or seeing her smile in person.

Even at night, there was no real rest. There was no sound in the desert except for the distant hum of cars and the occasional crackle on the radio. Trevor would lie on his cot, helmet off, and look up at the tent's ceiling while thinking about her. He knew she was in her last year of college, working hard, and probably feeling some of the same fear and worry he was feeling. Every time he thought of her, he became more determined to get through this and come back to her.

The Brave Rifles moved steadily through their assigned area, securing important roads, checking checkpoints, and carefully talking to the people who lived there. Every day, the regiment's discipline and training were put to the test, but Trevor's confidence grew with the responsibility. He was now a Cavalry Scout in the middle of a real combat operation, part of a mission that was much bigger than himself.

Even in the heat, dust, and stress, the thought of Alyssa reminded him that he was there to protect a future worth coming home to, not just to serve his country. Every patrol, every inspection, and every tense radio conversation held a silent promise: he would come back to her no matter what. That promise kept him calm, focused, and ready for the challenges that lay ahead.

The first part of their deployment was very important because it set the stage for the bigger conventional campaign. As the convoy moved forward, Trevor felt a mix of adrenaline, focus, and an unspoken determination: to serve, protect his fellow soldiers, and keep Alyssa in his thoughts no matter what happened next.

Alyssa,

I can't help but think of you while I'm sitting in this tent and the wind is blowing sand around outside. I miss you more than words can say. I keep picturing you on campus, walking between classes and laughing with your friends. It makes me smile, but it also makes the pain in my chest worse. I wish I could be there with you to hold you, see you, and share those times with you in person.

I wanted to write this, so you know what's going to happen and what to expect while I'm gone. I will be stationed here with the Brave Rifles for 11 months. We won't be able to do the little things we used to do on weekends, talk late at night, or even see each other for almost a year. I know it sounds long, and I know it will be hard for both of us. I've already thought about how hard it would be to leave you behind a thousand times, and I can only imagine how hard it is for you.

There is a lot of work, focus, and responsibility here every day. I stay sharp by doing patrols, checking vehicles, and getting constant training. But when I'm sitting in the Bradley and looking out at the desert for miles, I feel the distance the most. I think about you all the time. Every memory, laugh, and look we've shared gives me strength. I want you to keep in mind that this distance is only temporary, that this deployment has a purpose, and that I will be back with you.

I promise to write, send letters, and call when I can. I want us to share as much of ourselves as we can, even if we're far apart. I know it won't be as nice as being together, but it's the best we can do for now. Please remember that you are my anchor, my reason to keep going, and the thing that keeps me going the most. This deployment might be hard for us, but I'm sure our love can handle it.

Take care of yourself, work hard in school, and remember that it's okay to ask your friends for help when things get tough. Every day I'll think of you and count the days until I can see you again.

All my love, now and always,

Trevor


Hi Trevor,

I got your letter today, and I read it over and over, holding it like it was a lifeline. There are no words to say how much I miss you. It feels like something is missing every day without you. I keep thinking about the weekends we spent with each other, the long talks we had, and the quiet times we spent just holding each other. I never knew how much those little things would mean to me until now.

It hit me harder than I thought it would when I heard that your deployment would last 11 months. I won't lie; it scares me. I'm scared and worried about all the things that could go wrong while you're gone. I know you're trained and ready, but it's still scary to think of you out there, in danger, without me by your side. I just don't want to think about a day without you.

I also get why you're there and what you're doing. Trevor,

I'm so proud of you for being brave, dedicated, and willing to serve your country. I just wish there was a way for me to be with you, hold your hand, and let you know that you're not alone. I want you to know that I'm with you in every thought, prayer, and heartbeat, even though I can't be there.

I promise to stay strong for you and for us. I'll stay busy with school and rely on my friends when things get tough, but I'll never forget you. I'll count the days, remember every moment, and picture the moment we see each other again. And when that day comes, I'll be ready to hug you and never let go.

Trevor, please be safe. Come back to me. I love you more than I can say, and that will always be true.

With all my love,

Alyssa


Trevor was sitting in the small, dark tent while the wind blew dust across the compound outside. The patrol that day had been long and stressful, and for the first time in hours, he was alone and quiet. He pulled a small, worn envelope from his duffel bag. It had Alyssa's handwriting on it, which he recognized.

His heart raced. He opened the letter with care, almost as if he were praying, and began to read. As he read, a mix of love, longing, pride, and relief flooded through him. He could picture her face, hear the tremor in her voice, and feel the warmth of her hug as if she were right next to him.

He didn't care that his eyes were stinging with tears. He held the letter to his chest and felt the connection that stretched across thousands of miles. Her fears were the same as his, and her desire was the same as his. But there was strength in her words: a promise to stay strong, keep going, and wait for him. It gave him a reason to live and a way to stay grounded in the chaos of deployment.

Trevor leaned back against the canvas wall, read the lines again, memorized them, and answered them in his head. I'll be back with you. No matter what, I'll make it through this. I'll always have you with me, every day and every moment.

For a short time, in the middle of the heat, dust, and uncertainty, the war seemed a little easier to deal with. The letter was more than just paper; it was a lifeline, a reminder of home, and the reason he kept going through every patrol, every challenge, and every long, lonely night.

Trevor carefully folded the letter and put it in his uniform pocket, near his heart. He shut his eyes and said softly, almost to himself, "I love you, Alyssa. I'll be back. I promise."

Operations in western Iraq never stopped. The regiment did reconnaissance missions across large areas of desert, security patrols through towns and villages, and targeted operations against the last remnants of Saddam Hussein's regime. The aviation parts of the Brave Rifles took over a captured airfield, secured it, and kept control of it until July, when the 82nd Airborne Division took over. Trevor and the other soldiers quickly learned that to win in the desert, they had to be alert, flexible, and work collectively, because threats could come from anywhere, from IEDs on the road to insurgents hiding among civilians.

In addition to combat operations, Trevor also did civil military operations, which are a different kind of military duty. The Brave Rifles were one of the first units to arrive in the province, so they had to find a balance between being ready for battle and reaching out to the people who lived there. Soldiers interacted with civilians, protected important services, and worked to make the area safe so people could start rebuilding their lives. This was a new way of doing things for Trevor. It required patience, diplomacy, and cultural awareness, all while being aware that danger was always close by.

In August, the regiment started to focus more on governance and working as one. The 3rd ACR helped set up Al Anbar's first provincial council, which was a first for the province. Tribal leaders from all 60 major tribes were invited to work with U.S. troops and the new Iraqi government. Each tribe sent a sheik to represent them. Trevor watched the delicate talks and saw how diplomacy and military presence worked with each other. He learned more on this mission than he ever did in training. He realized that the mission was not just about fighting, but also about building a stable and self-sufficient society.

By September 2003, the regiment had taken control of most of the province, but Fallujah and Ramadi were still hotbeds of insurgent activity. Many patrols were tense, dangerous, and stressful for Trevor. The city was different from the open desert; they had to check every street corner, building, and crowd for possible threats. The 3rd ACR stayed in charge of these areas until the 3rd Brigade of the 82nd Airborne Division took over later that month.

During those months, Trevor learned how to do his job in ways that training could never have prepared him for. The mix of combat operations, civil military engagement, and seeing leadership decisions made in real time put his skills, resilience, and patience to the test. Every day was a reminder of how important the mission was for both the soldiers and the civilians whose lives were connected to it. And through it all, the thought of Alyssa kept him grounded. She was a reminder of home and the life he was fighting to get back to.

After weeks of tough patrols and long days in the heat of the desert, Trevor finally got a rare moment to himself. He was told he could call home for 20 minutes. He could only make one free call a month, which was worth $40, but it was a lifeline he couldn't afford to miss. His heart racing, he picked up the phone in the small communications tent, dialed Alyssa's number, and counted the seconds until he heard her voice.

"Hey Alyssa?" he said as soon as she picked up, his voice breaking a little from relief.

"Trevor!" she cried softly, and he could tell from the way she spoke that she was both excited and worried. "I've missed you so much."

He said, "I've missed you too," and then he closed his eyes for a moment to let her voice sink in. The noise of the desert around him, the distant hum of cars, and the faint chatter of soldiers seemed to fade away. It was just the two of them for these twenty minutes.

Trevor told her about the days and weeks he'd spent patrolling, the heat, the long hours of being on guard, and the strange mix of stress and routine. He told her about the missions they'd gone on, the villages they were helping to stabilize, and the little things they did that made them feel good about themselves. "It's hard," he said, "but we're doing everything we can to keep things safe." The Brave Rifles are still going strong.

Alyssa listened quietly, asking questions and laughing softly at the stories he told. He could tell she was worried, but hearing her voice made him feel better too. He leaned closer to the phone and spoke in a serious tone. "I know it's hard to be apart, but I want you to know that everything will be fine. I'm okay. I am careful. And I'm coming back to you."

There was a mix of relief and longing in her voice. "I just... I hate that I can't be there with you. Every day, I worry."

Trevor took a deep breath and fought to keep his anger and homesickness from taking over. "I know, Alyssa. I worry too. But we need to hang on. Every day we are apart brings us one day closer to being with each other again. And when we are, we'll make up for all this time. I promise."

The minutes went by too quickly, and soon the operator told him that his call time was almost up. Trevor clenched his teeth and enjoyed the last few minutes. "I love you, Alyssa. Please be strong for me and know that I am always thinking of you."

She whispered, "I love you too, Trevor. Please be careful."

The line went quiet and the call ended suddenly, leaving Trevor holding the receiver for a moment longer and looking at the small communications box. He put his hands over it and felt the pain of missing her, but he also felt a new sense of purpose. Every patrol, every mission, and every day in the harsh desert brought him one day closer to home and to her.

Trevor sat on the edge of his cot, still holding the phone. The sun was setting and painting the desert in shades of orange and red. The short talk made him feel both better and worse. He missed her more than he could say, but hearing her voice and knowing she was safe gave him a new sense of purpose.

Camp sounds were all around him: the distant hum of cars, the quiet chatter of soldiers finishing their work, and the faint clatter of tools. But for Trevor, all of that was secondary to the thoughts racing through his mind. He thought about Alyssa walking around campus, going to class, and living her life. He promised himself he would go back to her. Every patrol, every convoy, and every long night in the desert was for her.

The deployment was just starting, and the problems that lay ahead were too big to imagine. But Trevor felt a quiet confidence growing inside him, a mix of love, training, and experience. He had been tested before, but this time it was different. It wasn't just about duty or staying alive. It was about going back to the person who held his heart and gave him the strength to get through the hardest days.

He held his helmet tightly and looked at the dusty horizon. "I'll make it back to you, Alyssa," he whispered. "No matter what."

The desert night settled around him, big and quiet, but Trevor felt a steady spark of hope and determination inside him. The mission would go on tomorrow, the patrols would go on, and the Brave Rifles would keep going, but tonight he held on to the one thing that mattered most: the promise of going back home to Alyssa.

# CHAPTER FIFTEEN

*F*rom October 2003 to February 2004, Trevor and the 3rd Cavalry Regiment kept working in Al Anbar Province, which had changed from open desert to a complicated and unpredictable place of urban guerrilla warfare. The conflict had changed a lot since the first conventional campaign that overthrew Saddam Hussein's government. Now, it was mostly about insurgents, ambushes, and improvised explosive devices. Every patrol, every checkpoint, and every time they interacted with a village required them to be on the lookout, be flexible, and think quickly. Trevor quickly learned that no two days were ever the same. The quiet times between missions were few and far between, and they were only short breaks to write letters, check on Alyssa, or think about the lives they were trying to protect.

The Brave Rifles had more duties than just fighting. Stabilization operations involved protecting towns, helping civil military efforts, and working with local leaders to build trust and cooperation. Trevor saw firsthand how hard it is to find the right balance between using force and diplomacy to keep people safe while trying to build a working provincial government. These months required fortitude and forbearance, as insurgent threats were erratic, and the dangers to both soldiers and civilians were perpetual.

The 3rd ACR had been in Al Anbar for almost a year, by March and April 2004. They were replaced by a new Army Stryker Brigade and the I Marine Expeditionary Force, who took over the province. The Brave Rifles, also known as Task Force Rifles during the deployment, got ready to go back to Fort Carson, Colorado. At the end of the first deployment, there was relief and pride, but also a heavy sense of loss. During those months, fifty brave soldiers from the regiment had died, which was a sad reminder of how much it costs to serve. Trevor missed his dead friends a lot. He knew that the success of their mission had come at an unimaginable cost.

The regiment made sacrifices and faced difficulties, and their amazing performance was not overlooked. The 3rd Armored Cavalry Regiment got the Valorous Unit Award for their bravery, dedication, and professionalism during dangerous and stressful situations between April 25 and September 18, 2003. As Trevor got ready to go home, he felt both proud and sad. He knew that every patrol, every choice, and every mile he traveled had changed him as a soldier and as a person.

Going back to Fort Carson was the end of one chapter and the start of a new one. He would always remember the desert, the patrols, the letters to Alyssa, and the memories of fallen friends. He would also always want to be with the woman who had been his rock during the deployment.

The trip back to Fort Carson after almost a year in Iraq

felt like a dream. When the plane landed, Trevor's stomach twisted with relief, excitement, and the weight of everything he had been through. He was done with the desert, the patrols, the long hours on convoy routes, and the memories of friends who had died, but their effects were still very strong in his mind. As he walked through the terminal, he thought about how much he missed the simple things: the air in Colorado, the quietness of the mountains, and most importantly, Alyssa.

His heart raced as he stepped outside the airport and looked around at the people. He saw Alyssa standing there, looking around until her eyes found his. In a flash, the distance was gone. Trevor ran toward her, his boots hitting the pavement hard. When he got to her, he hugged her tightly. She held onto him as if she would never let go, and he held on just as tightly, breathing in the smell of her hair and feeling the warmth of her body against his.

His voice heavy with emotion Trevor whispered, "I missed you so much."

Alyssa said, "I missed you too," and tears streamed down her face. "I was so worried."

They stood there for what felt like forever, just holding each other and letting the fear and doubt, the months of being apart, fade away. Though there was a throng of people at the airport, at that moment, it was just the two of them.

The drive back to her dorm room was quiet as they took in being together again. Trevor held her hand tightly and sometimes brushed his thumb over hers as a silent promise that he was finally back. After months of worry, Alyssa leaned into him and put her head on his shoulder, letting herself feel safe.

As soon as Trevor and Alyssa got to her dorm room and closed the door behind them, all self-control went out the window. They held onto each other, clothes fell to the floor and were kicked aside. They couldn't wait another second. Their lips met in a fierce, desperate kiss, their hands roamed, their hearts raced, and the months of being apart led to a flood of passion.

They tumbled onto the bed, wrapped up in each other, the world outside the dorm forgotten. Every touch and hug was a powerful confirmation of their love, their desire, and the happiness of being in each other's arms again. As they moved, lost in each other, their laughter and whispered words mixed with heated gasps. They were reconnecting in the most intimate way possible.

They lay in the sheets, breathing heavily, hearts racing, eyes locked in quiet wonder at the fact that they were finally with each other again. Trevor held Alyssa close and traced soft circles on her back, promising her without saying a word that he would never let go. For the first time in a long time, everything felt right.

The next morning, the sun shone through the dorm window and made Alyssa's room look warm and golden. Trevor moved next to her, enjoying the rare feeling of peace and closeness, but there was still tension underneath it all. Every creak of the floor and every laugh he heard from far away made him tense for a moment, and his body reacted as if he were still on patrol. His heart raced, and even though he was safe in the room, he kept looking around, his eyes darting to the door and windows. A shadow of his time in Iraq that wouldn't leave him.

Alyssa moved next to him and put her arms around him, sensing something in the way he was sitting. "Trevor," she said softly as she brushed his hair back, "it's okay. You're safe. You're home."

He closed his eyes and let out a slow breath, telling his muscles to relax. "I know," he said in a low voice. "But it's hard. I still feel like I should be watching, checking, and staying alert here. "My body... is still in Iraq."

She held him tighter and put her head on his chest. "I understand. You've had a lot to deal with. Just let yourself breathe for a little bit."

Trevor nodded, trying to take in the comfort. He wanted to feel completely safe and present, but the war had left a mark that would last forever. Every patrol, every convoy, and every moment of being on guard had taught him to be ready for anything. Even though the dorm room was quiet, he kept thinking about what he saw, heard, and felt in the desert.

But as he felt Alyssa's steady heartbeat against him and the warmth of her arms around him, he let himself relax little by little. This was their home. This was love. He knew that the urge to scan and guard wouldn't go away overnight, but he also knew that with her by his side, he could slowly let go of the war that had been holding him so tightly and finally feel the peace of being back in the world he had been fighting for.

Trevor felt a mix of relief, excitement, and worry during the first few weeks back at Fort Carson. The desert, the patrols, and always being on guard had taken their toll, and he found it hard to fully relax. Even simple tasks like checking his gear, walking across the base, or sitting in the mess hall sometimes brought back memories of being on high alert in Al Anbar for months. His heart would race, and his hands would clench almost without thinking, a memory of war that wouldn't go away easily.

But there were times when he could rest. Getting back with his battle buddies gave him a sense of camaraderie and familiarity that made him feel grounded. Kowalski, Ramirez, and Jenkins were happy to see him again. They talked about what life was like on base while he was gone, teased each other, and laughed at old memories. Trevor liked the normalcy, the routines, the jokes, and even the little annoyances of life on post, but the shadow of his deployment never fully went away. He had to remind himself on purpose that he wasn't always in danger and that he wasn't patrolling dusty roads with insurgents hiding in the next building.

At the same time, his relationship with Alyssa became very important to him. They spent almost every weekend, going to local restaurants, seeing movies, and hiking when the weather was nice. Alyssa was kind and patient with him as she helped him get back into the swing of things at home. Trevor found comfort in her company, her laughter, her quiet confidence, and her ability to ground him when memories of Iraq came flooding back.

Even the smallest things had meaning. At night, next to Alyssa, he practiced letting go of the tension that had built up in him for so long as he listened to the steady rhythm of her breathing. He told her how he still felt uneasy and how his body reacted to threats. She listened without judging and always supported him. He slowly started to understand that healing didn't happen all at once; it was a slow process that was helped by the love and normalcy they shared.

Trevor's weekends with Alyssa were fun, but during the week he had to do his job as a Cavalry Scout at Fort Carson, which included taking care of vehicles, doing tactical drills, and training exercises. Life on base was structured in a different way and had its own set of demands, but it didn't have the constant stress of combat. He was able to start adjusting because he had a mix of routine and freedom. This helped him keep his skills and instincts sharp while he was overseas.

A few weeks in, Trevor had figured out how to balance his work, reconnect with friends, and enjoy his time with Alyssa. He would always remember the war, but he was slowly learning that being home with the person he loved was just as important to his survival. There were still going to be hard times in the months to come, but for the first time in a long time, he could breathe, laugh, and hope with a sense of grounded optimism.

# CHAPTER SIXTEEN

May 2004, University of Colorado Springs

*T*he morning air was cool and fresh, and the smell of just cut grass drifted across the UCCS campus. Alyssa moved the mortarboard on her head for what felt like the hundredth time. The stiff square was pushing against her temple. She nervously twisted the tassel with her fingers as she looked around at the growing crowd. Parents held cameras, friends hugged and laughed, and professors shook hands to congratulate each other. She had thought about this day for years, and now that it was here, it was so real it was almost too much to handle. There was a mix of pride and relief, along with a little bit of worry and nerves about what would happen next.

A shadow pulled at her heart even as happiness grew. Her father wasn't here in the crowd, and he wouldn't be. The pain of his absence after all the milestones he had helped her through made her throat tighten. She blinked away the tears and smiled.

She looked at Trevor, who was standing near the edge of the crowd with his hands deep in his pockets and his shoulders tense. The wind messed up his dark hair, and for a moment, she saw the slight crease in his forehead that showed he was worried. He saw her and moved closer, putting a comforting hand on her shoulder.

"I see him in you," he whispered. "He'd be proud. And I am, too."

Alyssa breathed out slowly and leaned into him. His steady presence gave her something real, warm, and unchanging to hold on to when she was sad. She said softly, "I just wish he could have been here."

"I know," Trevor said softly, lifting her chin until their eyes met. "We'll honor him together today, tomorrow, and every day after that. You're not alone in this."

She focused on his words and let the comfort they brought wash over her. The sound of gowns rustling and footsteps echoing on the polished floors of the auditorium marked the start of the ceremony. There were speeches full of advice and encouragement, but Alyssa didn't pay much attention to them. She was sad and proud at the same time, thinking about her father and how much Trevor had always been there for her.

When her name was finally called, she walked across the stage with steady steps, feeling both the weight of loss and the joy of success. Her fingers brushed against the diploma, which was new and crisp and a sign of years of hard work. And through it all, Trevor's voice rang out clearly and louder than anyone else's: "That's my girl!" A smile pulled at her lips and tears threatened to fall for both her success and the father who could only watch from somewhere else.

After the ceremony, her mother hugged her so tightly

Alyssa could barely breathe. Friends and family teased her nonstop about finally "making it" and how grown-up she looked. Trevor stayed by her side, holding her hand. His quiet presence protected her from the playful chaos around her. He leaned close and whispered a joke in her ear, which made her laugh through her tears. She felt a little better, though.

Later, Alyssa let herself feel everything as they walked hand in hand across the sunny campus. She felt happy, sad, and hopeful. She stopped for a moment and looked up at the sky. "I miss him so much," she said softly.

"I know," Trevor said quietly, and put his arm around her. "But he's inside you, Alyssa. He would be smiling so big right now. We will always carry him with us."

Alyssa leaned into him, her heart full. She didn't know what would happen next, but for the first time, she felt ready to face it, not alone, but with the man who had always been there for her through thick and thin. No matter what happened next, they would handle it as one, hearts intertwined with the kind of certainty born of love and support.

The jagged rocks of Garden of the Gods glowed with fiery reds and oranges in the morning sun, and long shadows danced across the dusty trail. The air smelled faintly of pine and dirt, fresh and invigorating, and birds sang in the distance. Alyssa smiled and adjusted the straps on her backpack as she looked around. The tall sandstone formations never failed to take her breath away, even after all the times she had been there.

Trevor walked up next to her and his presence was both comforting and exciting. He gave her a nervous smile. She saw him fidgeting with the straps of his pack and he kept brushing his fingers against his water bottle. There was something unspoken in the tension in his shoulders, a quiet energy that made her heart race without her knowing why.

As they hiked along the winding path, Alyssa's laughter bounced off the red stone walls. Trevor told one of his usual dry, self-deprecating jokes. The warmth in his eyes was always there, grounding her, but today it had something else in it: a mix of excitement and doubt that made her heart race.

As they went around a sharp turn, they came to a lookout point that showed them the whole view of jagged spires and wide open spaces. The wind blew over the ridge and lifted Alyssa's hair around her face. She turned to Trevor and took a deep breath of the fresh mountain air. He wasn't looking at the landscape or the path ahead; he was looking at her. His hands shook a little, and his eyes had a softness she had never seen before. It made her stomach twist in anticipation.

"Isn't this amazing? Wow," Alyssa said, her voice breaking a little in awe.

"It is," Trevor said in a low, almost reverent voice. "But... it's nothing compared to you."

Trevor moved before she could say anything. He put down his bag and slowly reached into the pocket of his jacket. She gasped when she saw the little velvet box in his hand. Her heart raced in her ears, and the world shrank to this one moment.

Trevor knelt on the flat rock, the red spires of the Garden of the Gods rising behind him like ancient guardians. Even the wind seemed to fall silent, as if the whole world had stopped to watch. All she could see was him steady and unshakable, his eyes shining with hope, his voice warm with love.

"Alyssa," he said, her name like a promise and a prayer. "Life is unpredictable, and none of us know what tomorrow holds. But there's one thing you can always count on. When I give my word, I keep it. And I'm giving you my heart, every day, for as long as I live." He drew a breath, his hand trembling but sure. "Alyssa… will you marry me?"

Alyssa's breath caught, and her hands flew to her mouth. Her tears made it hard to see, but her laughter came through, light and full of wonder. "Oh my God, Trevor," she whispered, the words getting stuck as her heart filled with joy. "Yes. Of course!"

Trevor let out a sharp breath and relief spread across his face as he put the ring on her shaking finger. She couldn't wait another heartbeat, so she pulled him up and wrapped her arms around him. Their kiss was both fierce and soft, full of relief, love, and excitement for the promise they had just made.

The red rocks around them were quiet, like ancient witnesses to their vows. The world below was big and never-ending, but all Alyssa could feel was the warmth of Trevor's arms and the steady beat of his heart against hers. For the first time, forever didn't seem like a mystery. It seemed like a promise.

They stayed at the overlook, their foreheads touching. The ring's new weight shone on Alyssa's finger when the sun hit it. She couldn't stop looking at it, at him, at the moment that seemed both unreal and completely unavoidable.

Finally, she laughed and wiped her wet cheeks. She teased, "You were so nervous," her voice light and loving. "I thought you were going to wear a hole in the straps of your backpack with all that fidgeting."

Trevor groaned and ran a hand over his face. "Was it that obvious?"

She smiled and said, "It was painfully obvious you were nervous, even though I didn't know why." She looked around at the tall red formations and the sky that seemed to go on forever. "This is great."

He looked a little embarrassed when he said, "I've had the ring for weeks. I froze every time I thought about asking. I wanted the time to be... right. Not in a hurry and not distracted. Only us."

Alyssa's chest felt warm. She reached up, held his face in her hands, and kissed him softly. "You did more than right." You made it a story I'll always remember."

As they started to hike back down, Alyssa kept stopping to look at her hand and turn her fingers so the diamond caught the light. She laughed at how silly she was. She playfully flashed her ring in front of him and said, "I look like one of those girls who can't stop showing off their ring."

Trevor bumped her shoulder and said, "You *are* one of those girls."

They walked in step, laughing freely with each other. The nervous tension from earlier was gone, and a happy feeling bounced off the rocks around them. A group of hikers passing by saw Alyssa's smile and whispered their congratulations when they saw the ring. Alyssa turned red, and Trevor, who wasn't used to being the center of attention, said "thanks" in a polite way before pulling her close to his side.

"Look," she whispered as they went around a bend. "Even people you don't know can tell."

"That I love you more than anything?" he asked.

"That too," she said with a smirk. "But mostly that you're stuck with me now."

Trevor laughed, a deep, happy sound, and kissed her on the head. "Best choice I'll ever make."

The sun was getting lower by the time they got to the trailhead, making the rocks look deeper shades of red and gold. Alyssa took Trevor's hand and squeezed it. Her heart was still racing with excitement, but underneath the chaos was something more stable and calm, a certainty she hadn't known she needed until now.

They had promised each other they would be together forever, and for the first time, forever didn't seem scary. It was like home.

Their engagement glow stayed with them like sunlight on

Alyssa's skin, but telling their families and friends about it quickly brought them back into the messy, unpredictable world of opinions.

Alyssa's mom cried as soon as she saw the ring. She held her daughter's hand so tightly Alyssa thought the diamond might leave a mark on her palm. "Oh, sweetheart," her mother whispered, her eyes full of tears. "He's a great guy. Your dad would be very proud. So proud."

Alyssa's heart had hurt during graduation week, but her mom's words made her feel better. Her mother had been there that day, sitting in the bleachers with her hands clasped tightly in her lap. Her smile was both bright and shaky. Alyssa noticed the tears in her eyes as she walked across the stage, and she knew those tears were not just tears of pride; they were also tears of sadness. Every milestone made them think of the empty chair and the man who should have been there clapping the loudest. Alyssa felt her father's absence like a shadow behind the joy as her mother's tears fell on her cheek again.

Megan, her sister, was less sentimental. She crossed her arms and smiled when Trevor showed her the ring. "I hope you know what you're getting into," she said, looking back and forth between the two of them. "She won't budge."

Alyssa's mouth dropped open. "Megan!"

Trevor just laughed. "Don't worry. I can deal with stubborn."

Megan smiled and shook her head. "You should. You will have to answer to me if you mess this up… because she is my sister." Alyssa liked that her words were playful, but there was steel underneath. A protective streak she found a little annoying.

Alyssa's closest friends at UCCS acted just like she thought they would: they screamed, hugged, and teased her nonstop. That weekend at the coffee shop, they passed her hand around like it was a precious jewel.

Her friend Emly looked at the ring as if it were made of stardust and said, "You're way too calm about this. I would have passed out if Trevor got down on one knee for me."

Another friend joked, "Honestly, I'm surprised you said yes right away. I thought you would make him work up a sweat. Alyssa, you had the power!"

Their laughter filled the store, but underneath it all, they were really happy. Alyssa couldn't help but feel the subtle change in her mind that her path was going in a different direction than theirs. Their lives were still full of classes, tests, and parties, but hers was suddenly full of wedding plans and the promise of a future with someone else.

Trevor's side was harder to deal with.

When he called his parents in Illinois, his mother almost screamed with joy on the other end. "Oh, Trevor! Finally! You were going to let that sweet girl get away," she said. Her excitement made him feel better, but his father's reaction was quieter and more measured, almost hesitant.

His father finally spoke after a long pause. "Marriage is a big responsibility, son. Especially with the Army and deployments. Are you sure you can handle that much weight?"

Trevor gulped hard. The old doubt came back, the same old battle between love and duty. But then he looked at Alyssa, who was sitting across the room and laughing as she told her mom about the proposal again, he felt the certainty steady in his heart.

"I'm sure," he said with confidence.

Of course, his Army friends didn't have any problems with it. When he told everyone in the barracks, they all started hooting and whistling.

"About damn time!" One of them yelled. "We were beginning to think you didn't have the guts."

One person hit him on the back so hard he almost spilled his drink. "Looks like you're off the market, man. You should enjoy the last of your freedom!"

They teased him nonstop, but Trevor didn't mind. He rolled his eyes and smiled. Behind the jokes, he saw the looks of men who knew what it was like to love someone while serving and what it was like to leave someone behind. Even though their friendship was full of crude jokes, they still respected each other.

Alyssa and Trevor were lying next to each other that night and all the laughter, teasing, doubts, and congratulations mixed together.

Alyssa slowly turned the ring on her finger and said softly, "It seems like everyone has something to say."

Trevor said in a calm voice, "They always will. But in the end, it's just us. You and me. That's all that matters."

Alyssa leaned in closer and put her head on his shoulder. She still felt the pain of not having her father there at graduation, but tonight, with Trevor by her side and her mother's blessing fresh in her mind, it didn't hurt as much. She knew he was right in that quiet moment. People would always have opinions, but their love was unbreakable.

The hotel room was quiet, a calm spot after all the phone calls, hugs, and teasing. The bedside lamp cast a soft glow on the walls, and every time Alyssa moved her fingers, the ring on her hand turned into a starburst of light. She nestled against Trevor, the simple closeness filling her with love and a warmth that felt like home.

Her mind wandered to the day when her mother's tears made her own vision blurry, Megan's sharp teasing wrapped in protectiveness, her friends' screams, and Trevor's father's pause on the phone. It all swirled around her like echoes, a mix of pride, worry, and love.

Trevor drew slow, absent-minded circles on her arm. "Are you okay?" he asked softly, as if the room itself needed to be treated with care.

She turned her head toward him, and her lips brushed against the fabric of his T-shirt. "I think so. It's just... a lot."

He kissed her hair. "It will always be a lot. People will have their own opinions, but they can't make decisions for us. That's up to us. It's our life."

The words settled in her chest, giving her strength. She

reached out her hand and turned it so that the diamond caught the light from the lamp again. It was small and simple, but it held a promise bigger than anything she could put into words.

The sound of cars on the street below was muffled by the window, and inside the room, time seemed to slow down. Alyssa moved closer, putting her hand flat over Trevor's heart. His body was warm, steady, and familiar.

"They'll get used to it," she said softly. "Everyone will. It's us."

Trevor smiled against her forehead and kissed her again, this time more gently, as if to seal her words in place. "It's always going to be us."

Alyssa closed her eyes as he held her, the newness of their bond both fragile and fierce. Whatever the future might bring deployments, distance, or the clash of family and Army, they had already faced more than most. And somehow, even in its early days, their love felt strong enough to endure. The world could wait. For now, it was only them.

# CHAPTER SEVENTEEN

*T*he morning came too quickly. The pale sky above Colorado Springs stretched awake, painting the Rockies in soft lavender light. Alyssa stood by the airport terminal's wide windows, her suitcase at her feet, tagged and ready. She was going home with her mom and sister now that graduation was behind her, but her heart stayed stubbornly in Colorado.

Her mother and Megan hovered close, checking boarding passes and talking quietly about connections and gate changes. Their words drifted past Alyssa like background noise, muffled behind the ache in her chest. She wasn't ready to leave. Not yet.

Trevor stood beside her in his sharply pressed uniform, hands shoved into his pockets. To everyone else, he looked calm and solid, a soldier ready for whatever came next. But Alyssa knew better. She saw the tight set of his jaw, the restless shift of his weight, and the way his eyes never left her face, as if memorizing every detail before she disappeared into the crowd.

"I hate this part," she whispered, not daring to look at him.

"Me too." His voice was steady, but she heard the weight

he couldn't shake. "I wish I could be on that plane with you."

She turned toward him, and for a moment the terminal blurred away. "I know," she said, her throat tight. "But the Army…"

"…always comes first," he finished, not bitter, just resigned. He shifted closer, brushing his knuckles against her hand in the smallest of touches. Not quite contact, not in uniform, not in public, but enough to tether them.

Her mom's voice cut through the moment. "Alyssa, honey, we need to start going through security."

The lump in her throat burned. She bent to grab her suitcase, but Trevor's hand closed over hers. She froze, her eyes stinging.

"Write me," he murmured, almost pleading. "Even if it's just a line. I'll write back as soon as I can."

"I will," she said quickly, blinking hard. "Every chance I get."

Megan appeared with her carry-on slung over one shoulder. "Come on, sis. We'll miss the flight." She shot Trevor a look half teasing, half protective that said more than words could.

Alyssa stepped into Trevor's arms, their embrace short and careful but full of strength, of promise. For one brief heartbeat, the busy airport hushed around them. Then it was over.

She pulled back, forcing a smile. "I'll see you soon."

"You will," he said, though they both knew *soon* was a word the Army rarely honored.

With her mom and sister leading the way, Alyssa walked toward security. Just before the corner swallowed her, she turned back. Trevor stood where she'd left him, tall and unshaken, his eyes locked on her until the crowd finally broke their line of sight.

As she slipped off her shoes at the checkpoint and handed over her boarding pass, the reality hit harder than ever. She wasn't just leaving Colorado. She was leaving him behind. For the first time since Trevor had asked her to marry him, she felt the true cost of loving a soldier.

Trevor's mind always circled back to Alyssa during the long weeks of training exercises, early mornings, and late nights. Every letter she wrote and every call they managed kept him tethered to something more than uniforms and schedules a life waiting for him beyond the Army, a life he wanted as much as he wanted her.

Then, during a routine meeting, the words hit him like a weight.
"You're scheduled for a second deployment," the commander said, his tone clipped. "It

begins next month."

Trevor sat still, the reality sinking in. Next month. It felt both distant and dangerously close. His thoughts went straight to Alyssa her smile, her laugh, the promise in the ring she wore. He needed to see her before he left again, needed her warmth to steady him for what was coming.

By that afternoon, he had already filed for a week of leave and booked a flight back to Illinois. That night, when she picked up the phone, he didn't waste time.

"Alyssa," he said, his voice tight with both urgency and relief, "I'm coming home to see you." A pause, then softer, heavier: "I have news, and I think it is better I tell you in person."

The flight seemed to go on forever, and every hour that went by made him more excited. When he finally got there, the familiar sights of his childhood town greeted him: the neatly trimmed lawns, the worn sidewalks, and the smell of rain mixed with the faint smell of freshly baked bread from nearby bakeries. But he was already thinking about the house where Alyssa lived with her parents, which had become their safe place during his short leaves.

He drove up the familiar driveway and saw Alyssa on the porch. Her hair was loosely pulled back, and she was shielding her eyes from the afternoon sun with her hand. When she saw him, her face lit up, and for a moment, everything else, like the Army, the upcoming deployment, and the months ahead, faded away.

As he reached her, she stepped into his arms. Her eyes were happy, but her brow was furrowed with worry. "What is your news?"

"I'm being deployed again. Not until next month, but I need you to know this now. I wanted to tell you in person."

His voice was low and steady.

Her hand was on his chest, and her breathing stopped for a second. "Next month... it seems so far away, but it also seems so real."

"I know," he said, moving a piece of hair away from her face. "I wanted this week to be ours. I want to spend it with you. And I want you to know that no matter what, we'll get married when I come back. That's what I promise."

She held him, letting his words hold her down. "I know you'll be back. I believe in you. And I'm not going anywhere either. We'll make it through, just you and me."

Trevor held her tighter, remembering how warm she was and how sure she was in her arms. After a long pause, he finally told her what had been bothering him for weeks.

"When I get back..." his voice was full of hope and fear, "I'm really thinking about leaving the Army. I want to plan a real life with you, not one where we have to count leaves and deployments."

Her eyes softened and sparkled with tears that hadn't fallen yet. "Trevor... I'll be here. All the time. No matter what."

For a few quiet moments, they just held each other on the porch and listened to the town's distant hum fade away. Their love, promises, and the fact that they had chosen to be together in that small space made all their worries go away.

Next month would come, but right now it was just them.

When Trevor woke up the first morning at home, he could smell bacon and coffee coming from the kitchen. After months in the Army, his parents' house felt impossibly small. Every creak in the floorboard and every corner reminded him of a life before uniforms, deployments, and orders.

His father sat at the kitchen table with the newspaper open, the picture of calm and patience. "Morning," Trevor said as he poured himself a cup of coffee, trying to slip back into the familiar rhythm of home.

His father said, "Morning," and his eyes went up for a second. There was an unspoken weight in that look: worry, pride, and a father's warning that never left him.

Trevor cleared his throat after breakfast, feeling the weight he had carried across the country. He said simply, "I got orders. Second deployment. I'm leaving next month."

His dad slowly folded the newspaper, dragging out the silence. He finally said, "I thought it was coming. You do a good job, but... it's a lot, son."

Trevor nodded and swallowed hard. "I know. And... I've been thinking. When I get back, I'm really thinking about leaving the Army. I want to plan a life with Alyssa that doesn't involve counting days or leaves. I want to make a future with her."

His father leaned back in his chair, narrowing his eyes in thought. "That's a big decision. You've given four years of your life to the Army. But...I won't argue if you're certain. I just want you to be safe and happy."

Trevor's mom came in next, wiped her hands on a dish

towel, and hugged him in a way that seemed to give him all the comfort he needed. "We're behind you no matter what you choose," she said softly. "Please come back to us. Always."

He thought about the conversation all day, feeling both relief and the sharp edge of responsibility. He felt a little better after talking about how he felt, but he was also more aware than ever of the months to come, the deployments, the uncertainty, and how important the present is.

The rest of the week Trevor kept completely focused on every moment with Alyssa, every smile, every laugh, and every quiet hug. They walked hand in hand through the quiet streets of their small town, stopping at the little café she loved and laughing over spilled sugar packets and jokes they both told. They had a picnic in the park near Alyssa's parents' house where they could enjoy the warm afternoon sun. For hours, it was just the two of them, with no uniforms, schedules, or orders just love and stolen moments. He loved her with all his heart. He knew he had to go back to the Army in a few days, but for now, this week, the world was just the two of them. Nothing else mattered.

They sat on the porch swing at her parents' house in the evenings, shoulders touching, fingers intertwined. Trevor remembered how her laugh sounded, how her hair caught the light, and how her eyes softened when she looked at him. Each kiss was both soft and strong, a promise that no distance or deployment could break their bond.

Alyssa put her head on his chest one night after dinner. "I wish this week could last forever," she said softly, her voice muffled by his uniform shirt.

He kissed her on the head and said, "I do too. But even if it doesn't, we'll get through it. Nine months isn't forever, and when I get back, we'll start making our life."

She raised her head to look him in the eye and put her hand over his heart. "I know you will," she said softly. "I believe in you. And I'll be right here, waiting."

The airport was eerily quiet, which was very different from the warmth and chaos of the week he spent with Alyssa and his parents. With each step he took toward the gate, Trevor's duffel bag got heavier. The terminal's bright lights seemed empty compared to the sunlit porch of Alyssa's family home, the smell of her hair, the sound of her laughter, and the brief taste of a life he wanted so badly.

He hugged his parents one last time. Their faces were full of pride and worry. "Be safe," his mother said softly as she put her hand on his cheek. "And always come back to us."

"I will," Trevor said, making the words sound stronger than they were. His father's hand hit him on the shoulder with quiet authority. "We trust you, son. Just keep your head. And also, look after her."

Alyssa was at the small airport café, and her engagement ring sparkled as she held his hands. She said softly, "I'll be here," and her eyes sparkled. "Nine months... it will pass. I'll be here when you get back. We're going to get married."

Trevor put a hand on her cheek and remembered how soft, warm, and certain her gaze was. He said, "I promise. I'll be back. Always."

The announcement for his flight rang out in the terminal. Time started to move again. They held each other one last time, trying to hold back the hours, weeks, and distance.

He walked toward security with his heart racing and looked back one last time. Alyssa kissed him silently with her hand over her lips and her eyes on him until the crowd hid her from view.

The plane waited, like a cold reminder of reality. The roar of the engines and the vibration of takeoff brought back memories of the life he was going back to: orders, drills, and the deployment coming up in nine months. But deep down, he was sure: Alyssa was waiting for him. Their life was real. And nothing—no distance, no uniform, no mission—could ever change that.

Trevor closed his eyes and let the memory of the week carry him forward as the plane climbed above the clouds. He thought of the warmth of home, the laughter, and the soft brush of Alyssa's hand against his. The long days of training, the Army's constant demands, and the hard work of getting ready for deployment were all ahead. But deep down, hope stayed with him, steady and unshakable.

He'd return for now, train, and deal with the deployment. And when the time was right, he would come back.

# CHAPTER EIGHTEEN

April 2004, Baghdad

*B*aghdad was a messy mix of concrete and sand-colored buildings with a dry, dusty heat that seeped into every bone. Trevor no longer noticed how hot his helmet got here with the sun beating down on it. The city was always full of tension from the buzzing of helicopters overhead to the gunfire in the distance amid the low, constant hum of Bradley armored vehicles rolling over bumpy streets. He'd flown into the middle of South Baghdad just a few days ago, and now, the weight of the mission felt like the desert itself.

Their goal was Tal Afar, a city known for its insurgent activity. The Brave Rifles were given the nearly impossible task of keeping it from spreading. They were to take back the city, neighborhood by neighborhood, house by house, and then somehow making it better than they found it. Engineers and soldiers worked collectively to build a huge berm around the city. This wall was meant to keep the insurgents inside while letting civilians leave safely. Trevor saw families with children and quickly packed bags pass by sandbagged checkpoints, their eyes nervous. He felt bad for these civilians because he knew violence would soon sweep through their streets.

The "clear, hold, and build" doctrine wasn't just military talk; it was life and death. Trevor's unit moved in an orderly way, clearing each neighborhood with methodical, often violent, door-to-door sweeps. Every door, every alley, every corner was a possible ambush for the unsuspecting. The violence was tiring, both mentally and physically, but there was an eerie rhythm to it that the soldiers had learned to follow.

Working with Iraqi soldiers gave Trevor both hope and frustration. The local forces knew the city well, but communication wasn't always clear, trust had to be earned, and there was always the fear of betrayal in every look. Trevor saw Iraqi police lead troops through the narrow streets, pointing out which homes were empty and which ones were hiding insurgents. The coalition and Iraqi forces started working slowly and painfully.

There were information operations going on at the same time as the gunfights. People handed out flyers and shouted messages from armored cars. This campaign wasn't against the people; it was for them. When Trevor saw civilians cautiously nodding or children peeking out from behind crumbling walls, their wide eyes showing both fear and curiosity, he felt a strange mix of cynicism and hope.

The toll was clear by the end of the first month. More than eight hundred militants had been captured and more than two hundred had been killed. The city started to show signs of life beyond the chaos: markets reopened, electricity flickered back on, and schools cautiously welcomed children who had missed months of classes. Trevor, on the other hand, knew better than to let himself be hopeful. He had seen enough to know that every gain in Tal Afar came with a cost, and those who refused peace could take back any street they cleared.

The human cost was still very high, even when they were winning tactically. By then, forty-three of their friends were gone, and the invisible cord around the hearts of those who were still alive was getting tighter. Every time Trevor passed a freshly dug grave or a row of empty bunks, he was reminded that success always comes at a cost.

And still, the Brave Rifles kept going, leaving their mark on the city. They were fighting not just for land, but for the fragile promise of stability in a place that seemed almost made to resist it. Trevor tightened his grip on his rifle and looked out over the horizon where dust met concrete. He wondered if the city would ever really be free or if their victories were just short breaks in an endless storm.

The morning air was full of dust as he and his team walked down a narrow street with low, sand-colored houses on both sides. Every step Trevor took on the cracked asphalt felt like walking on hot coals. Windows were dark, and doors were either tightly shut or hanging off their hinges. Sometimes, a child's head peeked out from behind a wall and then quickly disappeared. The city was cloaked in the kind of quiet soldiers know masks danger.

They had been told over and over again this wasn't just a sweep. Every house could be a trap. The city was full of threats you couldn't see until they happened: improvised explosive devices, snipers, and hidden fighters. Trevor's heart raced and his palms were sweaty against the grip of his rifle. He had been trained for this, but nothing he learned during the long hours at Fort Hood or in South Baghdad could have prepared him for the smell of gunpowder, dust, and decay.

"Clear right!" Sergeant Martinez yelled, and the squad spread out. Trevor kicked open the door to the first house with a spray of dust from his boots as he crossed the threshold. The air inside was thick and stale with the smell of burned cooking oil. He swept the room with his rifle, every nerve on edge. Nothing.

He crept forward. Another empty room. Suddenly a scuffle above alerted Trevor and his reflexes kicked in. He jumped to the side when a small explosion went off in the stairwell, sending dust and pieces of wood flying. The squad fired back, filling the house with the sound of M4 rifle fire. Trevor felt the kick of his gun, and the recoil calmed his mind even though adrenaline rushed through his veins.

In the middle of the chaos, the Iraqi soldiers moved forward, exchanging a silent signal. A young Iraqi private, who was only a boy, led the way up a staircase and pointed to a dark corner. Trevor followed. He crouched down and raised his rifle at the rebel hiding behind an overturned couch, his eyes wide with fear. The private nodded to Trevor, who held off on pulling the trigger right away. The most important thing was to catch him alive.

Hours went by like this, door after door, street after street. The line between the hunted and the hunter grew blurry, and every sudden noise—a falling pot, the scrape of a boot, a distant shout—made Trevor's stomach turn. But there were also signs of normalcy. A woman in one courtyard gave bread to the soldiers. Children ran and laughed between abandoned cars on another street, not knowing or maybe not caring about the violence going on around them. These little things felt weak, like the first buds of spring trying to grow through dry ground.

By nightfall, the team had gathered on a rooftop to look over the area. The sun went down, and the city turned orange and gray. Trevor's chest heaved, and his muscles were sore from being on guard for so long. He looked down at the streets and saw the burned-out cars and blocked-off alleys. Somewhere down there, insurgents were still planning, civilians were still praying, and his fellow soldiers were waiting for the next push, some of whom were still alive, and some of whom had already died.

For a moment, he lowered his rifle and breathed slowly. The wind brought him the sounds of Tal Afar: the distant rumble of armored vehicles, the faint Arabic chatter of Iraqi partners, and the gunfire that never really stopped. Trevor let himself think something for the first time since he got here. Something that was both scary and necessary to recognize: this city would change him. The question wasn't if, but how.

My Dear Alyssa,

When I sit down to write to you, I feel both closer to you and painfully far away. The days here are long and never-ending, full of noise, dust, and stress I've never felt before. But even in the middle of all this chaos, I can't stop thinking about you. I can see your smile, hear your laugh, and feel your hand slipping into mine when I close my eyes. It feels like nothing could ever keep us apart.

Alyssa, Tal Afar is very intense. Fear and resistance seem to be everywhere on the streets. We carefully walk through neighborhoods, house by house, always on the lookout and ready to go. Some days it seems like the city is holding its breath, and every noise, shout, or explosion makes my heart skip a beat. But then I think of you and how much you believe in me, and somehow, I find strength I didn't know I had.

I miss you more than I can say. I miss how your hair smells after a shower, how your hand fits perfectly in mine, and how warm your hugs are on quiet nights. I miss the little, perfect times we had together that made life feel safe and whole, even when we were just joking around. Being here makes me realize how much of myself is in you, Alyssa, and how empty everything feels without you around.

I promise you this: your love is like armor for me every day I am here. It keeps me steady when everything else around me seems shaky. And when this deployment is over— and it will be—I promise I want to come home and hold you until you can feel the months we've been apart melting away. I want to make up for every moment, every laugh we missed, and every touch we didn't get.

Until then, please know I am always thinking of you. You should know I am as safe as I can be. I'm fighting not just because I have to, but because I want to come back to life with you in it. Alyssa, you are my heart, and nothing here can ever change that.

Always, all my love,

Trevor


Dearest Trevor,

I got your letter yesterday and read it over and over, holding it to my chest like I could feel you here with me. I smiled and hurt at the same time with every word you wrote. I can't tell you how much it means to me to know you are thinking of me even in the middle of all that chaos. Because, Trevor, my mind is always on you.

I picture you walking through those dusty streets, alert and brave. My heart swells with pride and breaks a little with worry. I can feel your hands on your rifle and your eyes scanning every corner, but I also picture you thinking of me, which makes me feel closer to you than miles and danger could ever let me. I wish I could be there to hold your hand, tell you you're safe, and remind you that you are my home no matter where you are.

Words can't even begin to describe how much I miss you. I miss your laugh, your warmth, and the way your soft voice makes everything feel right. The nights are the hardest. I lie in bed and picture your arms around me, feeling your heartbeat next to mine. I swear it's the only thing that makes me sleep. When I close my eyes, I try to remember this is just a season and we will be again soon. Every moment apart will be worth it.

Trevor, I want you to come home to me. I want to make up for all the time we've spent apart. Until then, carry my love with you as I carry yours. Let it give you strength and hope. Remember that someone is waiting for you with open arms, a full heart, and love deeper than the desert sky where you are fighting.

My love, please come back to me safe. I'll always be here for you, waiting.

With all my heart,

Alyssa

Just like any other morning, the sun shone down on Tal Afar and dust blew through the streets. As Trevor's team moved carefully through a block of closely packed homes, clearing each one in order, the first shot rang out with a loud crack that was too close for comfort.

"Contact front!" someone yelled. Trevor crouched down and looked down the street in front of him. The morning light mixed with smoke and dust, making the alley look gray. He could barely see through the haze, but he saw movement: Sergeant Martinez charging forward to cover a corner. He yelled something and then fell down in a sudden spray of fire.

Trevor stopped for a split second, unable to believe what he was seeing. Martinez was more than just a leader; he was a friend who had been with the squad during drills, patrols, and every other tense moment since they arrived. Trevor ran forward, dodging debris and gunfire. His stomach tightened as he reached for the sergeant. The man's eyes met Trevor's, wide and full of disbelief. He reached out a hand, but it fell limp.

"Stay where you are! Fire back!" Trevor yelled at the squad, his voice sharp even through the lump in his throat. He shot without thinking, each bullet a mix of fear, anger, and helplessness. A cold numbness came over him. The fight didn't last long, but the sound of it stayed with him like a heavy weight on his chest.

Trevor knelt next to Martinez after the insurgents were driven away or were at least retreating. It was the first time he had felt the heavy reality of death in battle. The sergeant's face was calm now, almost peaceful in its finality, but Trevor couldn't shake the images, the fire, the suddenness, and the feeling of being helpless. It reminded them that winning in Tal Afar came at a price, and sometimes that price was too high to measure.

That night, Trevor sat alone in the temporary compound and looked up at the pale desert sky. He couldn't sleep. His hands were shaking. He kept going over the day in his head, the sights, the sounds, and the way Martinez had looked at him in those last few seconds. He felt a heavy, unending wave of guilt and sadness wash over him. He thought about Alyssa, her letter, and how much she believed in him. He wanted to tell her everything: how scared he was, how sad he was, and how much smaller and weaker he felt than he had ever thought possible, but he couldn't find the words.

Trevor knew something changed inside him during that moment with Martinez, when he saw how fragile life is and how quickly death can come. Now a heavy responsibility had taken the place of the confident soldier, the trained and ready warrior. He gritted his teeth and said softly into the night, "I'll take care of this, Martinez. I'll make it worth it. For you. For her."

The loss sparked something deep in him: a determination not to let fear control what he did or let the shadow of death take over their mission. Tal Afar had taken a friend, but it had also carved into Trevor's heart the heavy truth of what it meant to fight, stay alive, and hold on to the love waiting for him at home. Losing Martinez made him stronger.

Dear Alyssa,

I don't even know where to start. Today... we lost someone I loved and trusted with my life. Sergeant Martinez didn't make it.  I can't get the picture of him falling out of my head. The gunfire, the dust and smoke, the way time seemed to slow down, and the fact that the world kept moving around me were all so real.

Alyssa, I feel different now. A part of me is still the soldier, trained and ready, but another part of me is just a man who misses you so much and wants to go home where it's safe and normal. I've learned something cruel and lasting today: no amount of training can prepare you for losing someone you trust.

But I still reach for you even in this darkness. The only thing that keeps me steady is thinking about your smile, your laugh, and how warm your hand is in mine. It helps me get through streets that feel like minefields, both physically and emotionally. I wish you could be here to hold me for a little while to remind me there is still life outside of this mess.

Alyssa, I miss you more than ever. I miss the little things, like our quiet talks, your teasing smile, and how you make me feel like I can breathe when everything else is too much. I want to come home to you, hold you close, and never let go. But until then, I keep your love close to my heart like a shield, which gives me strength when I'm scared and feel like I'm being attacked from all sides.

Alyssa, I promise you that I will get through this. Not just for me and my brothers in arms, but for you too. I think of you with every heartbeat and every step I take in these streets. I fight so that one day I can come home and live a life where we don't have to say goodbye for so long.

Please keep me in your heart as I keep you in mine. I really need that thought right now.

All my love, and then some,

Trevor


Dear Trevor,

I just read your letter, and I can't even begin to describe how it made me feel. My heart hurts for you, Sergeant Martinez, and everything you've had to deal with over there. I wish I could take all your pain and fear and hold it in my arms so you wouldn't have to deal with it by yourself. I know I can't, though, so I'm writing to you to let you know that my heart is always with you, no matter how far away or dangerous it is.

Trevor, I can only picture the streets of Tal Afar, with all the smoke and dust and the constant stress. I can't see

Sergeant Martinez falling, but your words make me feel like I was there. I want to reach through this letter and hug you, whisper that you are safe with me in my thoughts and that I'm holding you steady when everything around you seems crazy.

I can't stand how much I miss you. I miss the quiet nights, the way we laughed, and how you made the world feel safe and full of possibilities just by being there. It's hardest at night when I'm in my childhood room, hearing the wind through the trees, and wishing I could feel your hand in mine. I pray for your safety all the time, and I hope that every time you start to feel scared, you can picture me standing next to you and telling you that you are stronger than the chaos around you.

Trevor, please promise me that you will keep going. Please promise me that you will take care of yourself and not let this darkness take more than it has to. Yes, fight, but remember that you fight for your life, for the love waiting for you at home, and for all the dreams we still have to live together. Soon, all of this fear, dust, and sadness will be behind us. I'll be there to hold you, laugh with you, and remind you that love is stronger than war.

I love you, Trevor. More than the distance, more than the fear, more than anything else in the world. Come back to me. I'll be here in Illinois, holding our love like a light until you come.

Forever yours,

Alyssa

For the last time, the sun rose over Baghdad. It painted the desert in pale gold and orange streaks that made the city look almost peaceful, at least for a little while. Nine months had gone by. Nine months of dust and gunfire, heat and fear, and the constant beat of life in a war zone. Every street Trevor walked down, every alley he cleared, and every home he went into had an effect on him. Tal Afar and South Baghdad had asked for more than he could have imagined, and Trevor had given them everything he had.

As the convoy moved toward the airfield, Trevor's body felt both heavy and strangely light. Heavy from being on guard all the time, from months of patrols and firefights, and from memories that would never leave him. Light because he could finally see the end, because he would see Alyssa again, and because the world beyond these never-ending streets was real and waiting.

He watched as the familiar desert turned into the base's sprawling tarmac, with helicopters lined up like metal sentinels in the morning sun. The soldiers moved with the practiced precision of people who had seen too much and lived through it, and Trevor let himself smile a little. He had made it. Most of his brothers-in-arms had lived through it. He thought about Sergeant Martinez and the other people they had lost, and the weight of their absence hit him again. But he also remembered them, which reminded him of bravery, loyalty, and the price of duty.

The horizon changed as they flew west, from sand to green, then from dust to clouds. Trevor put his head against the window and closed his eyes. He imagined Alyssa waiting for him, her hand reaching out, and her smile brighter than anything he had seen in the last fifteen months. He could almost hear her voice, feel the warmth of her touch, and the softness of her hug. He let himself hope for more than just survival for the first time in a long time. He hoped for a life after this war.

Getting back in the United States felt like a dream. The air smelled different, cleaner, and the sounds of life cars, voices, and birds were almost shocking after hearing only the sounds of fighting for so many months. Families rushed to meet their loved ones, hugging tightly, crying, and laughing, which broke the tension like sunlight breaking through clouds. Trevor walked through the crowd, looking for her. With every step, his heart raced faster.

Then he saw her. Alyssa stood just past the arrival gate, her eyes scanning the crowd until they found his. The noise, the crowds, the months of fear and being apart all went away. He ran, leaving his duffel bag and helmet behind, and she met him halfway with her arms outstretched. He held her so tightly that it felt like he could never let go. It was as if her warmth could make the months of war go away.

He whispered into her hair, "I missed you so much," and felt her tears on his cheek.

She said, "I missed you too," and her voice shook. "Trevor, you're home. You're finally home."

They held each other for a long time, letting the heaviness of being apart fade away and the fragile, unshakable joy of being with each other take its place. He was changed, and some of those scars would never fully heal, but when Alyssa held him, he felt peace, and a promise of the life he had fought to get back to.

The nine months of dust, fire, fear, and bravery were over. The chapter of war was over, and a new one, full of love, hope, and opportunity, was just starting.

# CHAPTER NINETEEN

February 2005, Fort Carson

*T*he February sun made the pale frost on the sidewalks shine, and the air was sharp and crisp outside from the last bits of winter. Inside the hotel room, the sun streamed through the large windows and warmed the quiet space. In this temporary world away from the noise and chaos, the dust, heat, and constant vigilance he left behind after fifteen months in Iraq, Trevor had a new appreciation for everyday comforts: a bed that wasn't a cot, a shower that didn't need careful rationing of water, and the soft hum of civilization outside the door.

Alyssa was with him now, but only for a week. She needed to return home soon to Illinois, where the wedding plans with her family were waiting. Trevor sat back and watched as she unpacked the small bag she brought, every simple movement filling the room with her presence. Her laughter came easily, wrapping around him and making the hotel feel like home, even after months apart.

They spent their mornings walking hand in hand along the quiet streets near the hotel, enjoying how easy it was to be with one another. They even made a little trip to a nearby café where they laughed over their coffee orders, joked about the people around them, and marveled at the simple pleasures of life that had once seemed normal but now felt like treasures. With each smile they shared, and each time Alyssa's hand brushed against his, Trevor felt the weight of the months lift a little.

During the afternoon, they planned the wedding. Color swatches, notebooks, and seating charts littered the bed in the hotel room. Trevor, who was still getting used to using a pen and paper, tried to keep up with Alyssa's detailed notes as they talked about ribbon choices, flower arrangements, and table layouts. There were small arguments about the color of the lavender for the bridesmaids' dresses or where to put the centerpieces, but it all ended in laughter and light teasing. Each argument reminded him that these were the kinds of problems he wanted to face with her for the rest of his life.

The hotel room was quieter at night, like a warm cocoon against the cold outside. Trevor traced circles on Alyssa's hand while they were wrapped in blankets on the small couch. Her voice was soft and soothing after months of letters and longing. Sometimes they didn't say a word, just let the silence hold them close. It was a simple way to be close after the war.

Trevor knew their week would go by too quickly. He didn't want to think about her going back to Illinois, but it was hard not to. Instead, he thought about the little, perfect things, like how her hair fell across her shoulder, how her hand fit in his, and how her laugh echoed through the hotel room.

Life back home was calm and planned, with small changes after months of fighting. Trevor had lived, yes, but now he had to learn how to live in a world where danger didn't control every heartbeat. He was willing to try for these few short days, with Alyssa by his side in a small hotel room in Colorado.

The drive to the airport seemed longer than it should have, but the sound of Trevor's truck rumbling under him was a little comforting. The worn leather seat still smelled like the desert, which reminded him of the months he spent in Iraq. Now, though, it felt like a way back home and to Alyssa. The February sun was low in the sky over the frost-covered fields of Colorado. She sat next to him, her hand resting lightly on his, silently reassuring him.

Neither of them said much. Words felt heavy, like they were too weak for the time they still had as one. Trevor stole glances at her profile, taking in the way her smile curved, the way her hair caught the light, and the quiet warmth of her presence next to him.

He parked his truck at the small airport and turned off the engine, sitting quietly for a moment before turning to her. He swallowed the lump in his throat and said softly, "I wish you didn't have to go."

Alyssa reached over and brushed away a piece of hair from his forehead. Her touch stayed. "I know," she said. "I'll be back soon. And until then, there are letters, phone calls, and wedding plans. Let's make it work."

Trevor leaned in closer and kissed her slowly and softly, remembering how warm and sweet she smelled. "Be safe on your flight, Alyssa," he said softly. "Let me know when you land."

"I will," she said, her voice shaking a little. "And Trevor, I love you."

He held her hands. "I love you too." Then he got her suitcase out and watched her walk toward the check-in counter. The sound of travelers and rolling luggage around her was familiar to him. She disappeared behind the glass doors. He felt a hollow ache in his chest that even the sound of his truck couldn't get rid of.

Trevor got back in his truck, started the engine, and felt the vibration under him. The drive back to Fort Carson was both familiar and strange. The base loomed ahead like a silent reminder of order, discipline, and the next stage of his life. He parked at the barracks, dropped his duffel bag by his bunk, and sat down on the edge of the bed. The room smelled a little like sweat and laundry, and the cold February air came in through the windows, cutting through the faint warmth of memories from the week with Alyssa.

He took out a small notebook and wrote to Alyssa as a way to stay in touch across the miles. He had to write down the details of the wedding, small personal notes, and plans for calls. This was as important a job as any he had done in Iraq. The deployment was over, but the work of rebuilding, adapting, and nurturing the life he wanted with Alyssa had just begun.

He leaned back and closed his eyes for a moment, picturing her waiting for him in Illinois and feeling the warmth of her hand in his again. The barracks was quiet, with only the sound of heaters and footsteps in the distance. Trevor felt steady for the first time in a long time. He was not just surviving; he was alive and ready to fight for life, love, and the future he wanted to share with Alyssa.

The next morning, Trevor drove his truck slowly along the winding roads outside Fort Carson. The cold February air cut through the cab and carried the faint smell of pine from the nearby foothills. The steady hum of the tires on the pavement gave him time to think and let the memories of Iraq and the excitement of going home mix together. He felt like he was getting a little bit of freedom back with every mile, but the weight of deployment stayed in his chest like an echo that wouldn't go away.

He parked at a quiet overlook and let his eyes settle on the valley below. The sun was setting, painting the peaks with soft gold and rose. From his backpack, he pulled out a notebook and gripped a pen. He could have called Alyssa, but writing felt more natural letters had been their lifeline during deployments, and the ritual still steadied him in ways a quick phone call never could. The words didn't come quickly, but they had to carry everything pressing in his chest: the longing, the relief, the fragile hope, and the gnawing doubt of whether he was truly ready to leave the Army behind.

Dear Alyssa,

I wish I could be with you right now, just sitting, talking about everything and nothing, and feeling your hand in mine. It's strange to be back in Colorado. After nine months of war, everything feels different, even though it's the same. The cold air and quiet streets make me think of how much I miss home, and more than that, how much I miss you.

It felt like we were with each other for a lifetime and a heartbeat during that week in the hotel. I keep replaying every moment, every smile, and every touch. It helps me get through the days until we're as one again. Life keeps going on, but I wish we could stop time and stay like this forever.

I have something to tell you, but I don't want it to scare you. In the next few months, I might be moving to Fort Hood, Texas. It's not set in stone yet, but it's on the table. I wanted you to hear it from me first because I want us to face it as one no matter where I go. We will figure out the wedding, the planning, and the life we are building. Distance is only temporary; you and I are not.

I can't stop thinking about the wedding, about us, and about the life we've always wanted. And I promise you this: I will do everything I can to get back to you, build that life, and make every moment worth the wait. I'll carry you with me in everything I do until then.

Alyssa, I love you. More than the distance, more than the fear, more than anything else I've ever known.

Yours always,

Trevor

A week later, Trevor moved through the rhythm of his day-to-day duties, still trying to find his footing after coming back from deployment. That evening, he stopped by the community mail room, shuffling through the stack of envelopes until one caught his eye Alyssa's handwriting.

He brought it back to the barracks and sat on the edge of his bunk. The soft light from a bedside lamp lit up her familiar handwriting on the folded piece of paper. He turned the envelope over in his hands before finally opening it. The familiar loops of her letters bridged the distance between them, making each word come alive in a way no phone call or email could ever capture. He traced his fingers across the page, holding on to the comfort of her voice written in ink.

Dearest Trevor,

I got your letter today, and I can't stop reading it over and over. Every word hurt me, but they also filled my heart. I wish I could reach through this page and hold you, feel your hands, and tell you that we'll face whatever life throws at us.

It was magical in Colorado, even if it was only for a week. Being with you again, feeling your warm touch, and seeing your smile in person reminded me of all the letters, calls, and times we had to wait during all the months you were in Iraq. I miss you so much now that I'm back home, but I will treasure those days.

Texas, Fort Hood. I read what you wrote, and I understand why it bothers you. I won't lie, the idea of us being apart again makes my chest hurt. But Trevor, I also know this: we've made it through months of letters, missing each other, and being far apart. We've been through more than most couples could ever think of. I know we can handle this as well. If moving to Fort Hood is part of your job and the life we're building, we'll figure it out.

I want you to think about the wedding, the plans, and the life that is waiting for us. And I promise you this: no matter how far apart we are or how uncertain things are, I will be here, waiting for you, loving you, and making our dreams come true with you. Being apart makes us closer to being together for real, every day.

You and I have both changed since you came home from deployment. But every change, every challenge, and every fear we face doesn't take away what we have. It makes it stronger. I love you more than I can say, more than words on this page could ever say. I will carry that love with me until I can be with you again.

Take care of yourself, my love. Always think of me the way I think of you. And remember this: no distance, no base, and no city can ever change how I feel.

Yours forever,

Alyssa

He took his time reading the letter a second time, enjoying every line. Her words were like a warm blanket around him, reminding him of the life waiting for him outside of the barracks, Fort Carson, and the echoes of deployment. "I've fought through more than most couples could ever imagine," she had written. He smiled. That was true. They had made it through being apart, not knowing what would happen next, and the long, painful months of letters and longing. He felt more stable now that he knew she was with him in spirit, even though Fort Hood was still a possibility.

Trevor leaned back against the headboard, folded the letter carefully, and held it to his chest. He thought about the drive to the airport, Alyssa's laughter, the warmth of her hand in his, and the times when they were alone in their hotel room. That week, that memory had become a lifeline. He already felt the pain of missing her, but the letter reminded him that their love was not limited by distance. It was strong, patient, and never gave up.

The idea of moving to Fort Hood made him uneasy. It would mean another change, another test of patience, and another stretch of uncertainty. But when Trevor read Alyssa's words, her promise to wait and her certainty that they could face it as one, he felt a quiet determination to settle in. They would be getting married in just a few weeks, then everything would be different. They would finally be able to live on base, no longer separated by rules and distance. Deployment had taught him how to be brave, strong, and to sacrifice. Life after deployment would demand the same, just in different ways.

He closed his eyes and pressed the letter to his lips. He whispered in a low, respectful voice, "We'll figure it out, Alyssa. We'll make it work no matter where I am."

The barracks around him felt less cramped now. The room was warmer, brighter, and almost alive with her love. Trevor could see the path ahead, even though it was unclear and winding. He was ready to take it one step at a time, with Alyssa waiting at the end. He carefully put the letter in his notebook, where it would be safe. It was a symbol of hope and devotion. For the first time in a long time, he let himself picture the life they would build, not just surviving, but thriving, side by side.

Trevor sat on the edge of his bunk with his phone to his ear. The barracks were quiet except for the distant hum of heaters and the faint sounds of soldiers moving through the hallways. He could hear Alyssa's voice right away. It was warm and familiar, like sunlight coming through a winter morning. It cut through the miles between Colorado and Illinois.

"Trevor! I just got the last word from the florist," Alyssa said, her voice full of excitement. "The bouquets are just right. Just like we planned, they'll match the color scheme perfectly: lavender, cream, and a hint of sage green."

Trevor smiled as he pictured her pacing around her parents' living room, her hands moving in animated ways. "That sounds great, Alyssa. I can't wait to see it all in person." He rubbed his thumb over the edge of his duffel bag, a nervous habit he hadn't been able to break since he got back from deployment. "I got my leave approved for the wedding and the honeymoon. That's two weeks in total. One for the cruise, one for the wedding."

"Oh my God, yes!" she said with a laugh. "I was hoping they would let you take time off. This is great; we can spend the whole week getting ready for the wedding without having to worry about anything else. After that, we can just relax on our honeymoon. No stress, no lists, just us and the ocean."

Trevor ran his fingers through his hair. "I can't tell you how much I've been looking forward to that. I just want to be with you, Alyssa, after everything. No barracks, no schedules, no letters or emails. Just us."

Alyssa's voice got softer, and there was a quiet sweetness in it that made Trevor's heart ache with desire. "Me too, Trevor. I can't wait to see you walk down the aisle and say, 'I do.' And the cruise... I've been thinking about that ever since you told me about it. It's going to be perfect: seven days of sun, waves, and no one else around."

He laughed, and the sound was low and sweet. "I just hope I can remember how to relax. I don't know how to turn off my high alert after it being on for so long."

"You'll figure it out," she said with confidence. "And I'll be there to remind you. We'll drink cocktails on the deck, put our toes in the sand, and every night you'll sleep with me instead of worrying about patrols or missions. You deserve it, Trevor."

Trevor's chest tightened with love and thanks. He said, "I've missed this," and his voice got quieter. "Just talking like this and making plans for our future. It's... it's everything I've been waiting for."

Alyssa laughed softly, as if she were shy. "Me too. It's hard to believe that in two weeks you'll be here, we'll get married, and then we'll go on the cruise. For so long, I've been dreaming about this day. Now it's almost here."

Trevor leaned back against the bunk and smiled, even though they were miles apart. "Almost real... That's how it feels after being apart for so long. Still… it feels more real than anything I've ever felt. Alyssa, I promise you those two weeks will be the best of our lives."

She said softly, "I believe you. I love you, Trevor. I'll see you soon."

"I love you too," he said, closing his eyes for a moment to let her words sink in. "I'll see you soon, my love. I can't wait."

Trevor put his phone down on the bunk and smiled slowly as excitement warmed his body. In two weeks, he would see Alyssa again, walk her down the aisle, and finally be free of the stress of deployment, even if only for a little while. He closed his eyes and thought about the sun shining on the deck of their cruise, her hand in his, and the sound of her laughter carried by the ocean breeze. For the first time in a long time, the future didn't seem uncertain; it felt like home

# CHAPTER TWENTY

March 2005, Saint Louis

*A*s they drove out of the airport, Trevor thought about how Alyssa had made the hour-long trip from her parents' house just to meet him at the St. Lous airport. The March air was cool with the first hint of spring. Alyssa's hand rested lightly in his, their fingers intertwining as they made their way through the familiar streets of St. Louis. Trevor's heart raced with excitement not only for their wedding this Saturday, but also for the rare, precious days they would have with each other before life pulled them back into routine.

"I can't believe it's finally here," Alyssa said softly, leaning her head against the seat. "This week is going to go by so fast."

Trevor smiled and quickly looked at her. "I know. But every second with you will be important."

The drive carried them out of St. Louis and into the quiet stretches of rural Illinois. Fields, still bare from winter, rolled past on either side, broken up by weathered barns and the occasional cluster of trees. As they crossed into familiar roads, Alyssa pointed out landmarks from home places woven into her childhood. Soon, they entered their hometown and turned onto the quiet street where her mother's house stood. The small two-story home sat with patches of frost lingering in the shaded corners of the yard. Alyssa eased into the driveway, and as they stepped out, he tightened his grip on Alyssa's hand, grounding himself in the moment.

Her mother was waiting on the porch to greet them, a warm smile spread across her face. Delicious smells wafted out the open door. "Trevor!" She hugged him tightly and said, "It's so good to see you."

Trevor smiled and hugged back. "Thank you, ma'am. This weekend can't come soon enough."

After years of barracks living and two tours in Iraq, being surrounded by the warmth of family and the smells of home-cooked food touched a chord deep inside Trevor. The chaos of war melted away and all he could think about was the new life he and Alyssa were about to start. They spent the night going over the last-minute details of the wedding, but managed to steal quiet moments, a brush of hands, a shared glance, a soft laugh. Reminders to remind each other that these two weeks were theirs alone after all the months apart.

Trevor finally leaned back in the living room chair and watched Alyssa move around while her mother sat nearby giving her soft advice. He knew that no matter what happened next—Fort Hood, another assignment, or the duties that awaited him after the honeymoon this week—this moment was theirs. And for the first time in a long time, he was sure that love, patience, and commitment could get them through anything.

The rehearsal took place in the small chapel near Alyssa's mother's house. The space was warm and inviting, with polished wooden pews and stained-glass windows casting soft colors across the floor. Friends and family filled the pews, chatting quietly as they waited their turns to practice. Alyssa's bridesmaids lined up at the side, whispering to one another with smiles that carried both nerves and excitement. Trevor's groomsmen stood across from them, adjusting ties and cracking lighthearted jokes to ease the tension.

Trevor caught sight of his parents sitting in the second row, his mother dabbing her eyes with a tissue while his father gave him a steady, approving nod. The sight made Trevor's chest tighten. This moment, this gathering, was proof of how close they were to forever.

When the officiant called them forward, Trevor's heart raced as he walked down the aisle with Alyssa for the first time. It wasn't the wedding day yet, but the nearness of it filled the chapel with anticipation. The officiant guided them gently through each step, explaining where they would stand and what they would say, words that felt familiar after so many letters, phone calls, and brief visits apart.

At the altar, Alyssa's hand slipped into his. She gave a soft squeeze, and when he looked down, her smile lit up the stained glass around them. He realized how much he had missed the rhythm of being with each other touching, holding, laughing quietly between them. "Are you ready for Saturday?" she whispered, her eyes shining.

"I've never been more ready," he said softly. The words were more than a promise; they were a quiet vow to himself that all the distance, letters, and months of deployment had brought them to this point.

After the rehearsal wrapped up, everyone made their way back to Alyssa's mother's house for dinner. The small home was filled with laughter and the hum of voices as the bridesmaids and groomsmen crowded around the table alongside Trevor's parents. Plates of food were passed back and forth, stories were shared, and the room buzzed with the easy warmth of family and friends coming collectively for something joyful.

Trevor found himself glancing at Alyssa often, watching the way she lit up when her bridesmaids teased her or when his parents told stories from his childhood. For a few hours, it felt like all the waiting, the distance, and the uncertainty of the past years had melted away.

As the night wore on, goodbyes were exchanged at the door. One by one, the bridesmaids, groomsmen, and Trevor's parents headed out, leaving the house quiet again. When the last car pulled away, Trevor and Alyssa were left standing side by side in the stillness, the nearness of Saturday hanging between them like a promise.

Later, Trevor was sitting by the window, looking out at the dark streets lit up by streetlights. Alyssa had fallen asleep on the couch with her head on the armrest and a soft blanket over her. He looked at her with a full heart and thought about all the things that had brought them here: the letters, the deployment, the long-distance calls, and all the little moments of waiting. Every hard thing he had to go through was worth it for this: a quiet, normal night with her by his side, the promise of a wedding in a few days, and the dream of building a life side by side, so close now.

He leaned back and slowly let out a breath, putting a hand on his chest where her heart would have been if she had been awake. He whispered softly to both the night and her, "Soon. Finally, it's us. And that's all that matters."

Trevor woke before the sun, the soft gray light of March slipping through the guest room curtains. He moved quietly through the still house and made his way to the kitchen. The room was silent except for the faint hum of the refrigerator and the slow drip of the coffeemaker. He poured himself a cup and sat at the table, wrapping his hands around the warm mug. Alone with his thoughts, he let the quiet settle over him, the calm before the rush of the day to come.

He slowly breathed in and ran a hand over his face. Today was the day he had been waiting for during his deployment: every letter, every call, and every lonely night apart. He felt a mix of nerves, excitement, and respect, but he also felt a steady warmth knowing that Alyssa was only a few rooms away.

He could hear her moving around in the hallway. She was talking to her mom about last-minute details in a soft voice. He put his hand on his chest and thought about how her smile would make her eyes light up when she saw him at the altar. The months apart had made him more grateful for these simple, every day moments that were so short-lived. Now they were about to become something special.

Trevor put on his wedding clothes carefully. They were crisp and new, unlike the rough clothes he wore on deployment. He remembered that this day wasn't about missions or schedules as he buttoned every button and straightened every crease. It was about love, commitment, and the life he and Alyssa were about to start.

Trevor grabbed his things before heading to the chapel. Tradition held firm he wasn't allowed to see Alyssa before the ceremony. Every difficult moment they had endured felt like it was leading here, to the moment he would finally see her at the altar.

At the chapel, sunlight poured through the stained-glass windows, spilling shades of blue, gold, and rose across the polished wooden pews. The air carried a faint sweetness from the lilies and roses arranged at the altar, their fragrance mingling with the old, comforting scent of polished oak.

Guests began filling the pews, their hushed voices fading to stillness as the music began. Trevor's groomsmen were already there, straightening ties and sharing quiet jokes meant to settle nerves. His best man clapped him on the shoulder, offering a grin that was half encouragement, half excitement. A few pews back, Trevor spotted his parents. His mother's eyes were already glistening, while his father gave him a steady nod, the kind of look that said more than words ever could.

Trevor stood near the front, shifting his weight as the minutes crawled by. The air buzzed with whispers, the shuffling of guests finding their seats, and the faint music of the organist warming up. He knew she was close. The next time the doors opened, it would be Alyssa walking toward him, and their lives would change forever.

Trevor stood at the altar, his hands hanging loosely at his sides. His chest was tight with nerves and excitement, but beneath it all was the steady certainty that this was the moment he had been waiting for... the culmination of months of waiting, writing letters, and longing.

Across the aisle, Alyssa's bridesmaids lined up in gowns of soft spring tones, bouquets clutched gently in their hands. Her sister, the maid of honor, held her head high, though her eyes already shimmered with unshed tears.

Trevor saw his mother press a tissue to her eyes, trying and failing to contain her emotions, while his father gave him a quiet nod of pride. Their presence grounded him, yet his thoughts kept racing ahead to the moment the doors would open.

And then they did.

Alyssa appeared, walking slowly down the aisle on her mother's arm. Her mother's steps were sure, but heavy with feeling, her face caught between pride and the absence of the man who should have been there. For a moment, Trevor's throat tightened, struck by the courage it must have taken for her to carry this role alone.

But then his eyes found Alyssa, and everything else fell away.

The lace of her dress caught the light in delicate patterns, the fabric flowing around her like something out of a dream.

Her bouquet trembled slightly in her hands, roses and baby's breath tied with satin ribbon. She looked radiant, her veil brushing her shoulders, her smile fragile and certain all at once.

Their eyes met, and for Trevor, the chapel, the guests, even the pastor waiting at the altar disappeared. There were no barracks, no deployments, no long nights writing letters by dim lamplight just Alyssa, walking toward him, closer with every step.

Alyssa paused with her mother at the end of the aisle, her bouquet trembling slightly in her hands. The lace of her dress caught the morning light and shimmered as though it belonged only to this moment.

The lump in his throat swelled as Alyssa and her mother began the walk forward. Each step seemed to carry the weight of every challenge they had overcome to stand here now. By the time she reached him, Trevor's chest ached with anticipation.

He reached for her hands, and the warmth of her skin made his own tremble. The simple act of touching her felt extraordinary, as if the world had finally caught up to the promises they had whispered in letters and dreams.

He whispered, "You look perfect," in a low but steady voice.

"You do too," she said, and the simple truth of it made his chest ache with happiness.

They said their vows to each other, and the words came easily, even though each one carried the weight of being apart for months, of wanting to be together, and of promises kept. Trevor spoke softly but with a lot of feeling, never taking his eyes off hers. He felt like every word brought them closer. When they said, "I do," he felt a rush of relief and love. This was the start of the life he had fought for and dreamed about many times while he was deployed.

As Trevor and Alyssa walked hand in hand to the reception, the chapel emptied out into the warm spring air. Laughter and congratulations followed them. The hall was full of noise from their families and friends talking, clinking glasses, and celebrating. Trevor felt a lightness he hadn't felt since before he went to war. He was so happy that it hurt his chest in the best way.

As they walked through the crowd, Alyssa leaned into him and held his hand tightly. She whispered, "I can't believe it's real. We're married."

Trevor kissed her on the forehead and smiled down at her. "It has always been real. We just finally made it official."

The reception was a blur of laughter, dancing, and stolen moments. Trevor spun Alyssa around the floor, laughing as her laughter rang out, clear and bright, filling every corner of the room. He saw their friends and family smile at them, but for Trevor, nothing mattered more than how warm Alyssa was in his arms, with her hand over his heart, steady and sure.

As the reception wound down and the last of the guests drifted out, Trevor and Alyssa slipped away from the hall. Upstairs, they changed out of their wedding clothes—Trevor into a clean shirt and slacks, Alyssa into a light dress that flowed easily with her steps. When they finally walked out, it felt like the first breath of quiet after a beautiful storm.

Their bags were already packed and waiting in the car for the honeymoon. On the drive toward the port city, the hours melted into laughter, playful teasing, gentle touches, and whispered confessions of love. Every mile seemed to carry them further from the weight of duty and closer to the promise of the life they were beginning.

The salty wind from the Gulf of Mexico blew through their hair on the cruise ship, and Trevor felt a rare, freeing lightness. There were no barracks, no schedules, no letters, and no distance between them. They were just floating above the ocean with the sun shining on the waves. He wrapped his arms around Alyssa and held her close, feeling the rhythm of her heartbeat match his own.

She said, "I could get used to this," and closed her eyes as she breathed in the salty air.

Trevor laughed softly. "Me too. But I don't think I'll ever get tired of being right here with you." He kissed her on the head and felt the weight of the last few months the deployments, the separation, the letters, and the long nights melt away in the salty breeze.

Trevor let himself just be there for the first time in what felt like forever. He let himself feel the joy and peace of the moment. The future was bright and full of promise, and finally, he and Alyssa could face it as one, side by side, with their hearts in sync.

As Trevor and Alyssa stepped onto the sun-warmed deck, the ship rocked gently beneath them. The horizon seemed to go on forever, and the turquoise water sparkled like jewels. The air was thick with the smell of salt and flowers from the tropical islands they passed. Every breath felt like freedom, the kind he had dreamed of since leaving Iraq.

He wrapped his arms around Alyssa and pulled her to his chest. The soft warmth of her body kept him grounded. "I can't believe we're finally here," she whispered, her voice barely heard over the soft sound of the waves.

He kissed her on the head. "Me either. It doesn't feel real, does it? It's like a dream we've been waiting to live."

They spent the day exploring the ship, laughing over drinks on the sun deck, stealing kisses in secret places, and walking hand in hand along the promenade. Every look, every touch, and every laugh they shared reminded them of the life they had fought to build. There were no letters to write, no calls to make from far away, and no deployment to worry about. The two of them were free to love each other completely, without holding back.

They rented small kayaks one afternoon to explore a quiet cove. They paddled through clear waters that showed off the bright coral below. Alyssa was the first to kick up a splash of water in his direction, laughter bubbling from her lips. Trevor wiped the drops from his face, grinning as her eyes sparkled with mischief. Her happiness was impossible to resist. "You started this!" he called back, though her radiant smile made it clear he didn't mind one bit.

He teased, "I learned from the best," and dipped his paddle to send a small wave her way. She laughed again, and the sound was light and full. Trevor felt a wave of happiness that he didn't know he could feel.

As the sun set, painting the sky in gold, pink, and violet, they found a quiet spot on the deck where they could lean against each other and watch the horizon. Trevor put his arm around her shoulders and pulled her close.

He said softly, "Alyssa, these two weeks... this life we're starting... I've been waiting for it my whole adult life. I promise you that every moment will be important. We will face whatever comes next."

She put her hand on his chest and felt his heart beating steadily, with her own heart beating in perfect time. "I know we will," she said, her voice full of emotion. "And I can't wait for every single day of it with you."

The waves whispered around them, and the warm breeze carried their laughter and quiet confessions into the night. Trevor felt the months of separation, the letters, and the deployment fade away for the first time in a long time. Instead, he felt the certainty of the life he and Alyssa were building, hand in hand, hearts aligned, and free to love without hesitation.

There was a lot of laughter and the soft sound of waves under them on the ferry ride from the cruise ship to the shores of Cozumel. The turquoise waters sparkled in the sun, making patterns on their faces. Trevor couldn't help but look at Alyssa, whose hair was blowing in the wind and whose eyes were shining with excitement.

"This place is amazing," Alyssa said, her voice full of wonder as she looked at the island's bright, coral-colored buildings, palm trees swaying in the light wind, and market stalls full of flowers, woven textiles, and handmade crafts.

Trevor smiled and put his arm around her shoulders. "Not as amazing as you," he said, and she laughed and pushed him playfully.

They spent the morning walking around San Miguel, trying the local food and stopping to look at handmade jewelry and brightly painted ceramics. Shopkeepers and people passing by smiled when they heard Alyssa laugh. Trevor felt a warmth in his chest that he didn't know he could feel so freely.

Later, they rented a small scooter to ride along the island's coastline. The wind whipped past them as they sped along the sunny roads, stopping at quiet beaches where the sand felt soft under their feet. Trevor held Alyssa in his arms and crossed the shallow waves. Her laughter sounded like music over the soft roar of the surf.

They stopped near a quiet part of the beach where the water was so clear they could see the coral reefs below. Alyssa smiled at Trevor as she dipped her toes into the water. "Come on," she said. "You promised not to hold back on this trip."

Trevor waded in next to her, the water lapping at his knees. For a while, they just floated, letting the current carry them, their fingers intertwined. The months of deployment, the distance, and the endless waiting all faded away into the clear waters, and he felt a deep sense of peace.

As the sun began to set, painting the sky with gold, coral, and lavender colors, Trevor pulled Alyssa close and put his forehead against hers. "I've dreamed about us like this for so long," he said softly. "And now that it's real, I don't want to let go."

She kissed him softly on the lips, and the warmth of her smile stayed with him as the light faded. "You won't," she said in a low voice. "We'll never let go. Trevor, this is only the beginning. Just the start."

The last morning of the cruise was calm, with waves gently lapping against the hull and the sun rising over the horizon in shades of gold and coral. Trevor and Alyssa stayed on the deck for a while, enjoying the last few moments of their honeymoon. The warm breeze, the sparkling ocean, and the fact that they could just be alone without any responsibilities or distance between them was very special.

They got off the ship and walked hand in hand back to land.

Soon the warm tropical air turned back into the cold air of March as they reached St. Louis. The drive to Alyssa's mom's house was peaceful and comfortable. Their hands were intertwined, and the car was filled with small talk about souvenirs and wedding memories. The house welcomed them like a hug. It was warm, funny, and quiet, just like family life after weeks of adventure at sea.

They took their time unpacking over the next day, remembering every item, every memory, and every joke they had shared on the trip. They walked through the rooms, with quiet smiles and gentle touches showing that the honeymoon was over and they were back in the real world. But even in the ordinary, there was magic in the two newlyweds enjoying their first days as husband and wife, loving and safe at home.

Finally, the day came when Trevor had to leave. Alyssa drove him to the airport, and the sun shone on her car as they held hands one last time. "I hate that you have to go," she said, her voice heavy with sadness.

Trevor said, "I know," and held her close for a long time. "But I'll be back before you know it." And then there was Fort Hood.

They kissed softly and slowly, not wanting to let go. "I'll be waiting," she said in a soft voice.

Trevor walked through the airport doors with a mix of determination and longing. He thought about their honeymoon, the warmth of their time, and the fact that they would face the next chapter, the move to Fort Hood, side by side, no matter how far apart they were. As he sat down on the plane and watched the city get smaller below him, he let out a slow breath, his heart full, knowing that the life they had dreamed of was just beginning.

## CHAPTER TWENTY-ONE

*T*he plane landed at Colorado Springs Airport. The late-morning sun made long shadows over the snow-covered foothills. Trevor held on to the armrest for a moment, letting the engines' hum fade as the plane rolled to a stop. The recycled cabin air carried only the faint tang of jet fuel that clung to his clothes, but even that was enough to remind him he was back in Colorado.

He went outside after getting his bags. The cool spring air brushed against his face and brought with it the smell of pine and the warmth of the city. He stopped for a moment, looked up at the sky where the mountains stood out sharply against the horizon. He could feel the weight of the past few weeks settle around him. For Trevor, the memories of the honeymoon, Alyssa's laughter, and the warmth of holding her close were still fresh, but they mingled with the weight of the responsibilities awaiting him back at Fort Carson.

He slid into the driver's seat of his truck, where the familiar leather and engine hum kept him grounded. He took a moment to think as he drove onto the highway and the city gave way to the rolling plains and the mountains in the distance.

The gates of Fort Carson came into view. The barracks,

the parade grounds, and the quiet hum of military life welcomed him like an old friend. Trevor parked his truck and took a deep breath. The sounds of distant drills, boots shuffling, and vehicles rumbling reminded him that this chapter of leave was coming to an end, but the life of soldier, husband, and partner was still going on, with each role blending into the man he was becoming.

Trevor parked his truck in the familiar parking lot at Fort Carson. The cool Colorado air carried the sound of training exercises in the distance. He felt the usual mix of relief and tension as he stepped out and stretched his legs after the long drive from the airport. He was relieved to be home, even for a short time, but he was also tense because he had things to do. He was done with deployment, but military life never really stopped.

He walked to the administration office with his duffel bag over his shoulder, ready for the usual paperwork and debriefings that came after leave. Instead, he got news that made his chest tighten.

The officer looked at the papers in his hand and said, "Trevor. You are supposed to move to Fort Hood, Texas. Orders for a permanent change of station. You'll report in a few weeks."

Trevor blinked, and the weight of it hit him. Fort Hood. Texas. Another step. Another change. He rubbed his face to try to calm the flood of thoughts about housing, logistics, and the life he was building with Alyssa.

"And... your spouse can live with you on base," the officer said, seeing how he looked. "They have housing available, including a two-bedroom apartment for married people. Everything should be ready when you arrive."

There was a mix of relief and excitement, with a little bit of fear. He could see it clearly now: Alyssa wouldn't have to stay in Illinois. She would be there with him, in their own home in a new city. The idea made him feel better, replacing his nervousness with excitement.

Trevor sat down in an office chair for a moment to let the news sink in. Deployment, wedding, honeymoon, and now a new base across the country. Life was moving quickly. But moving in with Alyssa didn't feel like a challenge; it felt like the next step in the life they were building.

As he drove back to the barracks that night, the setting sun in Colorado painted the mountains soft gold. Trevor thought about how their apartment at Fort Hood would be decorated, how they would start to form small routines, and how laughter would fill their new home. He smiled and tightened his grip on the steering wheel.

This was it. It was the start of a new chapter, but this time he wasn't alone. Alyssa would be there with him, and together they would deal with whatever came next: deployment orders, moves, and all the surprises life threw at them.

The days at Fort Carson went by quickly, with a lot of final briefings, packing, and planning. Trevor went back and forth between the barracks, the supply office, and the administrative building, checking boxes, signing forms, and making sure nothing was missed. Every task had a quiet weight to it. It wasn't just the physical effort of moving; it was also the mental burden of knowing that a new city, a new base, and a new life were waiting for him.

That afternoon, Alyssa pulled through the gates at Fort Carson after the long drive from Illinois. Her car was loaded down with clothes, boxes, and small comforts she wanted to bring for their new life in Texas. Trevor was waiting for her near the barracks, and when he saw her step out of the car, a smile broke across his face, chasing away the weight of orders, paperwork, and military deadlines.

For the next two days, Alyssa stayed in a hotel in Colorado Springs while Trevor wrapped up his duties and cleared out his barracks room. They packed duffel bags, folded uniforms into neat stacks, and crammed boxes into the back of his truck and her car. Even in the middle of the work, they found time to laugh Alyssa teasing him about how much gear he owned, Trevor sneaking quick kisses whenever she handed him another bag.

On their last evening in Colorado, Trevor walked her out to the parking lot beside the barracks. From there, the mountains rose against the fading light, the Rockies glowing gold in the sunset. They leaned against his truck for a while, her head resting against his shoulder.

"It's going to be different in Texas," Alyssa said softly, her voice touched with both excitement and sadness.

Trevor kissed the top of her head. "I know. But it'll be us. That's all that matters. Wherever we end up, we'll make it ours."

They stood in silence, holding on to the moment the memories of their honeymoon, the quiet days in Colorado, the laughter and warmth that had carried them this far. They didn't think much about the mountains they were leaving behind. What mattered was the road ahead, and the promise of facing it with each other.

That night, Trevor stacked his duffel bag by the door of his barracks room and lay awake for a long time, Alyssa asleep at the hotel just a few miles away. By morning, they would both leave Colorado. Trevor leading the way in his truck, Alyssa following close in her car as they headed south. Fort Hood was waiting, with new challenges, new routines, and new memories they hadn't yet imagined.

Trevor drove his truck onto the base at Fort Hood. The sun was high in the sky and the warm Texas air smelled faintly of mesquite and dust. It was a different world from the mountains and cool spring air of Colorado, but he could feel a quiet excitement building in his chest. Alyssa sat next to him, her eyes wide with interest and excitement as she took in the huge area that included the post, the parade grounds, the barracks, and the long lines of family housing apartments.

"This is big," she said softly, holding his hand. "It's a lot to take in."

Trevor smiled softly at her and laughed. "It is. But this is where we're going to live now. This is our first real home as a married couple."

They parked their truck outside their two-bedroom apartment and got out. The building was small and looked like a typical base housing unit, but to Trevor and Alyssa, it was the first step into their new life. They took boxes and suitcases up the short flight of stairs. Each item was a part of them: their clothes, honeymoon souvenirs, and little things that made the space feel like home.

Alyssa quickly got to work organizing, moving books and pictures around and carefully setting up the small kitchen. Trevor hauled in the heavier boxes, arranged the living room, and then moved through the apartment with the practiced eye of a soldier. He checked the locks on the windows and doors, tested the smoke detector, made sure the first-aid kit was stocked, and placed a flashlight and spare batteries within easy reach. They were the kinds of details most people overlooked, but years of deployments had trained him to notice them without thinking.

It took them a couple of days to get everything situated. Boxes were unpacked slowly, one at a time, the apartment gradually shifting from bare walls to a space that felt like theirs. The steady hum of the air conditioning filled the quiet, and the sounds of life outside seemed far away. By the second evening, the small living room had begun to look lived in, its quiet warmth making them feel safe and close.

Trevor leaned against the doorframe, watching as Alyssa placed a small picture of them into a frame on the shelf.

"You've already made it feel like home," he said softly.

She turned, smiling as she crossed the room and slipped her hand into his. "We're home.. That's all that counts."

Over the next few days, life found a comfortable rhythm. They ran errands on base, explored the nearby town, and unpacked the last of the boxes. Trevor handled base procedures, updated his paperwork, and met with his new chain of command. Alyssa arranged the furniture, added small touches to brighten the rooms, and even met a few neighbors who stopped by with warm smiles and quick introductions. Slowly, piece by piece, the apartment became more than just a place to stay. It became theirs.

There was a sense of peace underneath it all, even with the little things that were bothering me, like the new roads, the long lines at the commissary, and getting used to life on base. They were together, making a life that was only theirs.

At night, Trevor and Alyssa often drifted off on the couch or in bed, their arms wrapped around each other. They talked quietly about the future dreams of a home, children someday, and the life they might build beyond the Army. For Trevor, those conversations felt like something rare and steady, a calm so different from the constant deployments and the uncertainty that had shaped so much of his past. Lying there with Alyssa beside him, he realized he was finally beginning to imagine a life that wasn't defined by orders or duty, but by the woman who had waited for him, loved him, and was now his wife.

They had come to Fort Hood as a soldier and his wife, but they were also partners in every way, ready to face whatever challenges and joys awaited them in their new home.

The first week at Fort Hood went by quickly, with each day mixing the demands of military life with the small, everyday tasks of married life. Trevor got back into the rhythm of his duties, which included briefings, inspections, and meetings with his chain of command. However, this time there was a clear difference. With every choice and every step, he thought of Alyssa next to him, the quiet comfort that home wasn't just a room; it was her presence.

Alyssa moved into their apartment without any problems, making it a cozy, welcoming space that showed off both of them. The walls were covered with pictures from the honeymoon, a soft throw was draped over the couch, and little things in the kitchen made even the most boring tasks feel like rituals. She laughed when Trevor tried to make coffee one morning and spilled half the pot. He smiled sheepishly, glad to have someone to share both the little problems and the quiet victories with.

They went all over the base, from the PX to the commissary, and even found a little café where they starting going for breakfast on Saturdays. Trevor realized he had missed more than he could have imagined in these everyday moments: the shared smiles over scrambled eggs, the gentle teasing, and the comfortable silences. Deployment had taught him how to be patient and tough, but marriage was teaching him how to enjoy the moment.

In week two, they went on small adventures outside the base. They drove to nearby parks, found new places to eat, and drove along stretches of open Texas highway with the wind blowing past them. Every time they went out, they were reminded of their partnership, their shared excitement for life after deployment, and the life they were building with each other.

Trevor and Alyssa sat on the small balcony of their apartment one night as the sun went down and painted the sky gold and lavender. He put his arm around her shoulders, and she put her head on his chest.

"I never thought I'd feel this peaceful," Trevor said in a soft voice. "Even after all we've been through."

Alyssa tilted her head and smiled at him, making his heart skip a beat. "That's what love does, Trevor. It doesn't take away the bad times, but it makes everything else worth it."

He kissed her forehead softly and felt her warmth in his arms. "Then I guess we're right where we need to be."

As they sat in silence, the lights of the base twinkled below them, and the cool Texas night washed over them. Trevor had the deep realization that home isn't a place, it was Alyssa. And no matter where the next deployment, move, or challenge took him, they would take it on side by side, stronger, closer, and in love forever.

Trevor's mornings at Fort Hood started early, with the Texas sun already shining on the base as he put on his boots and went over his tasks for the day. Briefings, inspections, and training schedules gave life on base a rhythm, but now there was a new layer: Alyssa. Knowing she was only a short drive or walk away gave him a quiet sense of comfort, a reminder that he was no longer alone in the military.

That afternoon, while he was in the office going over paperwork and base rules, his boss called him in. The meeting was short, professional, and full of military jargon that Trevor was used to. Then came the news that made his heart race.

The boss gave Trevor a folder and said, "I need to tell you about the status of your contract. You have only six months left to serve. After that, you can choose what to do with your career."

Trevor stared at the paper, and the words slowly began to make sense. Half a year. It was both a relief and a shock to see a timeline that was real and tangible. He felt the familiar mix of duty and excitement. The deployments, the moves, the letters, and the distance had all brought him to this moment with Alyssa. Now that his time in the military was almost over, he was ready to go.

He stepped outside into the warm Texas air and let it wash over him. Then he called Alyssa. He told her the news when she answered the phone, and her voice was warm and curious.

"Six months," he said without any other words. "Then we can really plan." No deployments, no orders from the base. "Just us."

I could hear her laugh on the other end of the line. It was light and full of hope. "Wow, Trevor, that's great. I knew it was coming soon, but hearing it makes me feel free."

He smiled as he thought about her in their apartment, moving things around, planning meals, and adding little touches that made it feel like home. "Exactly. And for now, we enjoy living here. We'll make the most of these next six months."

That night, Trevor leaned against the doorframe of the apartment and watched Alyssa cook dinner. The golden Texas sunset came through the window and lit her up with a warm glow. He felt very thankful. He had to deal with unpredictable deployments, moves, and orders, but these quiet times full of love and laughter reminded him of what was most important.

Six months wasn't forever, but it was a promise, a chance for them to build a life, enjoy the comforts of home, and get ready for the future they both wanted. Trevor sat down at the little table in the kitchen and took her hand.

He said, "We've got six months of us," in a low but steady voice. "And then... the rest of our lives."

Alyssa smiled and held his hand tightly. "Six months, and then forever."

And for the first time in a long time, Trevor let himself really believe it.

After a long day of base work and paperwork, Trevor and Alyssa sat on their small balcony that evening. The Texas sky was full of sunset colors. The air was warm and smelled faintly of mesquite and barbecue grills from nearby neighborhoods. Trevor put his arm around Alyssa and pulled her close. He could feel the steady beat of her heart against his chest.

He said softly, almost to himself, "Six months," as he watched the colors change on the horizon. "After that, we get to make all the choices."

Alyssa leaned closer, her cheek brushing against his shoulder as her hand slid down to lace gently with his. Her voice was quiet but steady. "It feels like we've already climbed a mountain. But standing here with you now... I know the best part is still ahead, but we can make these next months ours, too."

Trevor pressed a gentle kiss into her hair, his smile lingering as he held her close. "We've earned this," he murmured, the weight of it grounding him. All the deployments, the endless miles, and the constant goodbyes were behind them now. With Alyssa beside him, the road ahead didn't feel uncertain anymore it felt alive, brimming with possibility, with joy, and with the kind of love that steadied everything else.

Trevor let himself breathe, really breathe, for the first time in years as the first stars appeared in the huge Texas sky. The road ahead was still unclear, and the military would still be a part of his life for a little while longer, but right now he and Alyssa were together, making a life that was theirs alone.

Holding hands and with their hearts in sync, they watched the night settle over Fort Hood, knowing they would face whatever problems came their way in the next few months. And in that quiet certainty, Trevor felt a peace no battlefield ever allowed. It was a peace that came from love, home, and the promise of a future that was finally theirs.

# CHAPTER TWENTY-TWO

October 2006, Fort Hood, Texas

*T*he heat in Texas stayed strong even after the sun went down behind Fort Hood. Trevor was sitting on the edge of the couch with his boots untied and his hands on his knees. Alyssa lay down next to him, barefoot in one of his t-shirts, with her hair still wet from the shower. The only sounds in the apartment were the hum of the ceiling fan and the faint laughter of soldiers' families coming from the courtyard outside.

Trevor leaned back against the couch, watching her flip through a stack of lesson plans she had saved from college. He reached over, brushed his hand along hers, and waited until she looked up.

"You know," he said carefully, his voice steady but thoughtful, "once we finish these next six months at Fort Hood, I think we should start looking at houses in that little town near our parents."

Alyssa tilted her head, curious. "The one just outside of where I grew up?"

He nodded, a small smile tugging at his lips. "Yeah. It's close enough that we'd have family nearby, but it's still quite good place to build something of our own. And it would give you the chance to finally use that teaching degree. I know the schools around there are always looking for good teachers."

Her eyes softened, the idea clearly sinking in. Trevor watched her expression shift half surprise, half excitement. For him, the thought carried more than just practicality. It was about roots, about choosing something steady after years of living out of duffel bags, barracks, and deployments.

He squeezed her hand gently. "Six months will go by fast. When we leave Fort Hood, I want us to have something to look forward to something permanent. A place that's ours."

Alyssa's smile widened, her excitement plain. "I'd love that, Trevor. I could finally teach, and we'd be close to home. It feels like the life we've been talking about for so long."

Trevor's chest swelled at her words. He could see it as clearly as she did. The quiet streets, the small yard, evenings that weren't measured in deployments or orders but in the simple rhythm of being together. The kind of stability that felt like a luxury after years of moving from base to base. He nodded slowly, the thought turning into conviction.

"I've been thinking, too," he said, his voice steady. "When we get there, maybe I could try to become a police officer. Something steady. Something that keeps us rooted."

"You can serve in a different way," Alyssa said, "but you still have to be home every night. Deployments are out, and so are goodbyes at the airport."

Alyssa's thumb brushed against his knuckles, and her eyes filled with tears. "It sounds great. A small kitchen, our own house, and maybe a dog. Me teaching at the school and you working for the department. Just a normal life."

Trevor leaned back and closed his eyes for a moment to let her words sink in. A normal life. After years of sand, dust, and adrenaline, the idea of mowing his own lawn or saying goodbye to Alyssa on a Monday morning before work sounded like heaven.

He opened his eyes again and smiled at her in a way that made him feel good. "Let's make it happen. You can't just dream about it anymore. We go home in six months. We get a house. Let's start over."

Alyssa leaned in and put her forehead against his, holding their hands tightly between them. "Six months," she said softly. "And then the rest of time."

Trevor kissed her softly, tasting the salt of her tears and the sweetness of her vow. For the first time, the future didn't seem like a far-off dream. It was real, close enough to touch, and they both owned it.

Life at Fort Hood settled into a steady rhythm, which Trevor hadn't felt in years. Every morning was the same: Trevor put on his boots and went to work while Alyssa made coffee, and the sun shone through the blinds in their apartment. They would find each other again by nightfall, sometimes tired, and sometimes restless.

One Saturday night, the laptop was open on their coffee table, with empty mugs and half a bag of chips all around it. Alyssa leaned forward, her eyes sparkling as she clicked through listings for homes for sale in Illinois.

She turned the screen toward Trevor and said, "Look at this one. Three bedrooms, a small yard, and it's only fifteen minutes from our parents' house."

Trevor leaned in and put his chin on her shoulder. "Needs a garage. Where else am I supposed to put my truck?"

She playfully swatted at him, but her laugh echoed through the room. "Fine, the garage is not up for discussion. You have to agree this porch would be great for summer nights, though."

They kept scrolling, sometimes laughing at crazy listings and other times stopping to look at homes that seemed almost within reach. Each picture and description added to the life they were already imagining in their heads.

Alyssa called her mom later that week and told her about their plan to move back. She was so excited she couldn't stop talking about it. Trevor could hear her mom's happy tears through the phone, and then she started asking questions: "When? Where? Do you know the name of the town? Oh, sweetie, this is the best news I've heard all year."

Trevor's parents were just as happy. His dad gave him good advice about mortgages and interest rates, and his mom's voice broke with happiness. "I can't believe you will both be home again. It will feel complete."

Alyssa wrote down school districts and circled job fair dates in a notebook during the afternoons when she wasn't on the phone. As she twirled a pen between her fingers one night, she said, "I think I'd like to teach sixth grade. Old enough to be interested, young enough to still believe in magic."

Trevor watched her with quiet pride, picturing her in front of a class with a smile that lit up the room. He leaned over and kissed her cheek, saying, "They'd be lucky to have you."

He had his own research all over the kitchen table: police department pamphlets, academy requirements, and pay scales. "It's not the Army," he said to her one night, sounding thoughtful. "But it still feels like service. And I would be home for dinner. Every night."

Alyssa reached across the table and squeezed his hand. "That's all I need, Trevor. For you to come back to me."

They didn't have glamorous days, but they were their own. Going to the commissary became a quiet adventure, and walking around the base at night gave them time to talk about their dreams. They made simple dinners, laughed at bad movies, and talked about their plans for the future, which was only six months away.

In those normal times, when Alyssa was drawing out her future classroom or they were laughing and arguing about which house was best, Trevor found a new kind of calm. It wasn't the excitement of battle or the heavy burden of duty. It was softer and more steady. It was home, and it was coming together in front of him.

The six months went by faster than either of them thought they would. Spring turned into the hot Texas summer, which turned into the long, golden days of early fall. Trevor no longer counted the days by missions or deployments. Instead, he measured time in small milestones: the day Alyssa's notebook filled with teaching applications, the day the bank approved them for a VA-backed mortgage using his service record and benefits, and the night they found a house listing they both kept returning to, as if it already belonged to them.

By the end of September, cardboard boxes started to pile up against the walls of their tiny apartment. Alyssa wrote "Kitchen," "Books," and "Bedroom" on them in neat handwriting. Trevor laughed when he saw the box that said, "Random Stuff," but inside, each label made him feel lighter, as if a chain was slowly lifting off his shoulders.

Their last weeks at Fort Hood were a strange mix of looking back and looking forward. Trevor finished the last of his out-processing paperwork on base. He turned in his gear and signed forms, each signature a reminder that his time in the military was ending. For the first time in years, he was going into the unknown without orders, deployments, or the Army telling him where to go next.

Trevor and Alyssa sat on their balcony for the last time one night after a long day of packing and paperwork. The Texas night was warm, with cicadas buzzing in the distance and stars scattered across the sky like salt. Alyssa dropped her head to Trevor's shoulder, "You know, I think I'll really miss this place. The memories we made here, not the heat or the dust. It was our first home."

Trevor wrapped his arm around her more tightly and looked out at the rows of apartments, the glow of TVs in the windows, and the sound of other couples laughing below. "Yeah," he said softly. "Fort Hood is where we learned how to live with each other, how to figure out who we are. But Illinois... that's home. That's where we both come from, and that's where we'll build the rest of our life."

Alyssa smiled and spoke softly but firmly. "I can't wait."

The next morning, the last box was taped shut and the final bag packed. Trevor loaded their things into the back of his truck, the slam of the tailgate echoing like a goodbye he wasn't ready to say. One by one, his buddies from the platoon stopped by, some clapping him on the shoulder, others pulling him into quick hugs, their jokes hiding the weight of parting. Alyssa's friends came too, gathering around her with smiles that wavered at the edges, offering last-minute advice and promises to visit.

The base looked the same as always: soldiers moving with purpose, flags snapping in the wind, the steady rhythm of Army life carrying on without him. But for Trevor, it all felt different. He wasn't one of them anymore. Not really. He was leaving this world behind to start another, with Alyssa at his side.

He got into the driver's seat and Alyssa was right next to him, her hand already on his. He took a deep breath and turned on the engine. The truck's rumble was steady, familiar, and grounding.

The road ahead opened up and led north toward Illinois as they drove away from Fort Hood. Toward family, careers, and the house they would soon call home. Toward a future that they could finally make their own.

Trevor looked at Alyssa. She wore a small, hopeful smile on her lips and in that moment, he felt the Army's weight lift from him for the first time in years. Something lighter and brighter was left behind.

He said softly, "Here we go," as if he were talking to himself.

Alyssa held his hand tightly. "Let's go."

And with that, they left Texas behind, taking with them not only boxes of things, but also a promise of everything that was to come.

# CHAPTER TWENTY-THREE

September 2006, Illinois

*T*he flat farmland in Illinois went on and on in every direction, with fields that were just starting to turn gold with harvest. Trevor opened the window of his truck to let in the cool fall air. The breeze brought with it the smell of cut corn and woodsmoke, which was so different from the dry Texas heat they had left behind. It smelled like home.

Alyssa sat up straighter next to him as the road signs became more familiar. "Almost there," she said, her voice full of excitement. She lightly held onto his arm with her fingers, as if to keep herself in the moment.

As the sun set and the sky turned soft shades of orange and pink, they pulled into her mom's driveway. Before Trevor even parked the truck, Alyssa's mom rushed out the front door with her arms wide open and tears already in her eyes, hugging Alyssa.

"Finally, home," her mother whispered as she held her daughter close. "And this time, it's for good."

Trevor smiled and stepped forward to hug her too. The warmth of family, which he was used to, pressed against him and took away the last of his road-weariness. After years of deployments, being far away, and living in temporary housing, it felt strange to be home, where the promise of stability was waiting.

That first week was a blur of talking and getting back together. Parents stayed up late at the kitchen table, telling stories and asking each other questions about their plans. Trevor and Alyssa smiled and said yes, they wanted to buy a house in the town next door; yes, Alyssa was applying for teaching jobs; and yes, Trevor was already looking into the city police department.

Trevor sat at the dining room table one night with his laptop open and looked through the police department's recruitment page. Requirements, academy dates, and physical fitness standards all seemed oddly familiar but completely new. This was a different kind of uniform that would let him protect and serve without ever having to fly to another war.

Alyssa worked on her teaching portfolio across from Trevor, printing resumes and writing cover letters. "I saw a spot for sixth grade," she said, looking up at him with a smile. "Just what I wanted, and it will start mid-year if I get the job."

Trevor leaned back and watched her for a moment, feeling proud of her. "You're going to be great, Alyssa. Those kids won't even know how lucky they are."

She shook her head and blushed, but he could tell that her eyes sparkled at what he said.

It was quieter at night here than in Texas. There was no base traffic, no distant cadence calls, just the sound of the wind rustling through the trees and the faint hum of crickets outside the window. When Trevor was lying in bed, he often listened to Alyssa's steady breathing next to him and thought about the house they would soon buy and the life they were already building.

It was no longer just a dream. It was happening, but slowly.

There were a lot of phone calls, showings, and disappointments in the next few weeks. Trevor and Alyssa spent their afternoons driving through the quiet streets of the town next door and parking in front of homes with "For Sale" signs in the yards. Some were too small, some were too old, and some just didn't feel right.

"This one has personality," Trevor said quietly one cold morning as he pushed open the creaking front door of a house with peeling paint. He ran his hand along the wood trim and thought about how much work it would take to make it livable.

Alyssa squinted and looked into the dark kitchen. "Character? It feels more like it's haunted. I want a house we can live in, not one we have to fix up."

They laughed, which broke the tension of the search for a moment. By the third week, they were starting to feel tired. Then, on a clear Saturday morning, their real estate agent took them to a small three-bedroom ranch on the outskirts of town.

Alyssa's shoulders relaxed as soon as she walked in. The sun shone through the living room windows and bounced off the walls that had just been painted. The kitchen wasn't very big, but it was comfortable and had enough room for the two of them to cook. Trevor ran his hand along the counter, and his heart was surprisingly steady.

"This feels right," Alyssa said in a whisper, her eyes wide.

He nodded, already imagining a grill in the backyard and maybe even a dog running through the grass. "Yeah," he said in a soft voice. "This is it."

The Army bonus had cleared Trevor's old debts, giving them a clean slate. Even then, getting pre-approved for a VA loan wasn't easy until Alyssa's mom stepped in to help with some of the upfront money they needed. With her support, the bank gave them the green light. Within a week, Trevor and Alyssa made an offer on a house. When the call came that their offer was accepted, Alyssa leapt into Trevor's arms, her laughter ringing through the empty rooms, already making the place feel like theirs.

"We have a home," she said, her voice thick with happy tears as she leaned against his shoulder.

Not long after their house offer was accepted, Alyssa got the call. She sat at her mom's kitchen table, gripping the phone, tears welling as she listened. Trevor was already leaning forward when she hung up.

"Well?" he asked.

She smiled. "I got the job. Sixth grade English at the middle school!"

Trevor yelled and hugged her, picking her up off the ground. "That's great, Alyssa. Just right."

She laughed, and her happiness spilled out. "Trevor, can you believe it? Our first home and my first real teaching job. It feels like our life is finally taking shape."

Trevor held her close and kissed her forehead. "You worked hard for it, Alyssa. And I'm going to work hard to get my place on the police force, too. Then we'll really be making the life we talked about."

For the first time, their dreams weren't just things they talked about in the middle of the night or wrote down in notebooks. They were real. A home. A job. A time to come.

They sat on the porch of her mom's house that night and watched the sun go down behind the trees. The world felt both familiar and new. They had known it all their lives, but now they were finally stepping into it as husband and wife, partners building their own home.

Now they were done with the Army and the war. There were classrooms, patrol cars, backyard barbecues, and the promise of normal days just like the ones they had been hoping for.

And neither of them would have given it up for anything.

When Trevor opened the application packet for the city police department, the house still smelled a little bit like fresh paint. He sat at their new kitchen table with a cup of coffee next to him and the sun shining on the papers. The questions were simple: work history, education, and references. But each line had a lot of meaning. This wasn't just another job application. It was the first step toward the life he had been dreaming about for months, one that meant coming home to Alyssa every night.

Alyssa sat on the floor with her legs crossed and stacks of brightly colored binders and lesson plan books all around her. She frowned as she wrote down notes for her first week of teaching. Her lips moved silently as she practiced how to introduce herself and the rules of the classroom. Trevor looked at her for a moment, and the corners of his mouth turned up. He had seen her dream about this for so long, and now she was just a few days away from being in front of her own class.

Without looking up Alyssa said, "You're staring again," in a teasing voice.

Trevor signed his name at the bottom of another form and said, "Can't help it." "I have the cutest teacher in Illinois as my wife."

She rolled her eyes, but her smile gave her away. "Officer-to-be, you should save that charm for your interview."

By mid-November, Alyssa began her new job at the middle school, stepping into a classroom mid-semester to cover for a teacher on leave. On her first morning, Trevor drove her to the building, watching as she nervously fidgeted with her lanyard and name badge. The parking lot buzzed with buses and students carrying backpacks, but the anxious energy belonged to her, it was Alyssa's first day. Before she got out of the truck, Trevor reached over and took her hand.

Trevor squeezed her hand, offering a steady smile. "You're going to crush this," he told her, meaning every word. She leaned in and kissed him quickly before slipping her bag onto her shoulder. Trevor watched her walk toward the building, noticing the nervous energy in her steps, the mix of fear and excitement she carried. His chest swelled with pride. This was Alyssa stepping into the life she had always wanted, and he couldn't wait to see her shine.

That same week, Trevor continued the process of applying to the police: physical fitness tests in the cool November weather, written tests in clean classrooms, and interviews that made him think hard about why he wanted to be a police officer. He thought of the Army with its rules and structure at every step, but this was different. This time, his goal wasn't to go to war or be deployed; it was to serve with roots, which meant keeping the streets where his family lived safe.

They were tired but happy when they got home at night. Alyssa told stories about students who were already trying her patience, a shy girl who opened up after reading aloud, and how excited she was to stand in front of her class. Trevor told stories about timed runs, doing push-ups until his arms hurt, and a panel of officers who watched every word he said.

"Do you think you'll make it?" Alyssa asked one night while they were curled up on the couch.

He kissed her on the head. "I've been through worse. But this time, I want it more. For us."

Alyssa smiled and traced lazy circles on his chest with her fingers.

"Then you will."

Trevor hadn't felt like this since he left the Army. His life was finally settling into a steady rhythm that he could shape with his own hands. Alyssa was teaching, he was chasing his new career, and they were finally writing a story that was all their own.

Trevor started the police academy application process with veteran expediency in early September. In November, he got his acceptance letter. He held the envelope in both hands for a long time before opening it, thinking about all the choices that had brought him to this point. Alyssa stood next to him in the kitchen, almost jumping with excitement. When he read the words, "Congratulations, you have been accepted into the police academy," her scream could be heard all over the house. She hugged him tightly, and as she did, laughter bubbled up in a mixture of relief and pride. "You did it!" she said, putting her forehead against his. "You really are doing it."

Trevor smiled, and his face looked softer because he was relaxed. "I guess I have to get used to getting up early and doing push-ups again."

The academy was hard. He started his days with physical training that pushed his limits and then spent hours in the classroom learning about state law, criminal procedure, and community policing. It made him think of the Army, but without the stress of having to go to war. He didn't have to deal with deserts and body armor; instead, he had to deal with traffic laws, radio codes, and hours of practice on the firing range. But at the core of it, the discipline felt familiar, like putting on a pair of boots he had worn in a different life.

Alyssa was getting used to the middle school. For the first few weeks, it was a mess. Students talked over her, homework was turned in late, and one boy tested her patience every day. Some nights she came home on the verge of tears, unsure if she had made the right choice. Trevor listened quietly and steadily, rubbing her shoulders as she talked.

Then, small wins started to show up. The girl in the back who was shy started to raise her hand. The troublemaker did the best work she had ever seen after being given the chance to lead a group project. Parents sent her emails thanking her for motivating their kids. Alyssa's confidence grew, and her classroom became a place she owned, not just put up with.

Their nights became sacred. They cooked dinner even when they were tired. Sometimes just a quick bowl of pasta, other times with Trevor out by the grill. Over meals they traded stories: Alyssa imitating the dramatic sighs of her sixth graders, and Trevor admitting how tough it was to memorize entire legal statutes or get corrected by his training officer during a traffic stop. They laughed, sympathized with each other's frustrations, and kept pushing one another forward.

On a Friday night in December, they sat on the small porch of their house with blankets around their shoulders. The air was cool and smelled like fallen leaves.

"Do you ever wonder where we'd be if I had re-enlisted?" Trevor asked in a low voice, looking into the dark.

His mind drifted to those long nights in Iraq in 2004, when Alyssa's letters from UCCS, filled with stories of her education classes and promises of a life with each other had been his anchor through the dust and danger. Those handwritten pages, smudged from rereading, kept him sane when the world felt like it was unraveling.

Alyssa leaned against him and her breath was warm on his neck. "I try not to. Because I would miss this. All of this."

Trevor kissed the top of her head, his chest tightening with thanks. Those letters he received in Iraq had pulled him back to her, to this moment, this porch, this life they were building. "I'm glad I came back to you. To this life."

She looked up at him and her eyes sparkled in the light from the porch. "Me too." Every day.

At that moment, when the world around them was quiet and still, they understood something deep. The fights were over, but the real work on the life they had always wanted to build was just beginning.

By December, Alyssa had found her stride, making it through the tail end of her first semester. No longer the nervous new hire, she was "Mrs. Alyssa," whose energy brought her classroom to life with laughter and stories. She had a talent for getting even the quietest students to talk and for turning grammar lessons into stories that stuck. Some days she came home beaming with pride, and other days she fell into Trevor's arms, exhausted but happy.

Trevor, on the other hand, had four months left with the police academy. The days were still long, with PT before dawn, legal briefings that made his head spin, and hours of tactical training on the mat or range. But this challenge had an end that promised roots instead of distance, unlike deployments. He saw a purpose in himself that was important: a way to serve and protect without losing Alyssa to the spaces between.

They drove through the snow-covered fields of Illinois on Christmas. Alyssa's hand was in Trevor's as his truck hummed down the highway. When they got home to their parents' houses, the kitchens were full of laughter and the familiar smell of cinnamon rolls. They spent time with both families, sitting around Christmas trees glowing with warm lights and the scent of pine, talking about their plans and tell stories about Alyssa's classroom and Trevor's police training. And even starting a family in their new home.

For the first time, those dreams didn't seem like far-off maybes. They felt like plans that were real, solid, and just around the corner.

Trevor and Alyssa were back at their small house on New Year's Eve, sitting on the couch with a blanket around them. The TV counted down the last few seconds of the year and people were yelling from Times Square, but it was quiet in their living room.

When the clock struck midnight, Trevor kissed her slowly and steadily, tasting the promise of what they had already built and the hope of all that was to come.

He whispered, "Happy New Year" against her lips.

Alyssa smiled and put her hand on his chest. "Happy New Year, Trevor. To us."

The fireworks on the screen flared, but all Trevor could see was the light in Alyssa's eyes, the glow of the life they had fought for and finally found. There was no sign of war on the horizon for the first time in years. There was only love, home, and the open road ahead.

And that was all.

♥

# ABOUT THE AUTHOR

**Colin Bradley** is a storyteller with a passion for weaving tales of resilience, sacrifice, and enduring love. Drawing inspiration from history, military service, and the strength of the human spirit, his writing blends sweeping drama with intimate emotion. *Hearts Against Odds* reflects his deep respect for those who serve, the families who wait at home, and the power of love to overcome even the darkest challenges.

When he isn't writing, Colin enjoys quiet evenings in Mississippi and spending time outdoors. His favorite hobbies include traveling with his family, fishing, and hunting. His work is dedicated to honoring both the extraordinary and the everyday heroes whose stories deserve to be remembered.

Readers can connect with Colin, explore more of his work, and follow his latest updates by visiting his website at www.colinbradley.com and checking out his social media.

www.ingramcontent.com/pod-product-compliance
Lightning Source LLC
Chambersburg PA
CBHW050311110726
47899CB00007B/2200